DRAGON THIEF SERIES

<u>SEASON ONE</u>
Dragon Thief
The Chicago Job
The Poisons Book Job
The Vault Job
The Femme Fatale Job
The Scavenger Job

<u>SEASON TWO</u>
The Crown of Kingship Job
The Green Scroll Job
The Payback Job

THE VAULT JOB
A DRAGON THIEF STORY

DRAGON THIEF
BOOK FOUR

KAT SIMONS

THE VAULT JOB

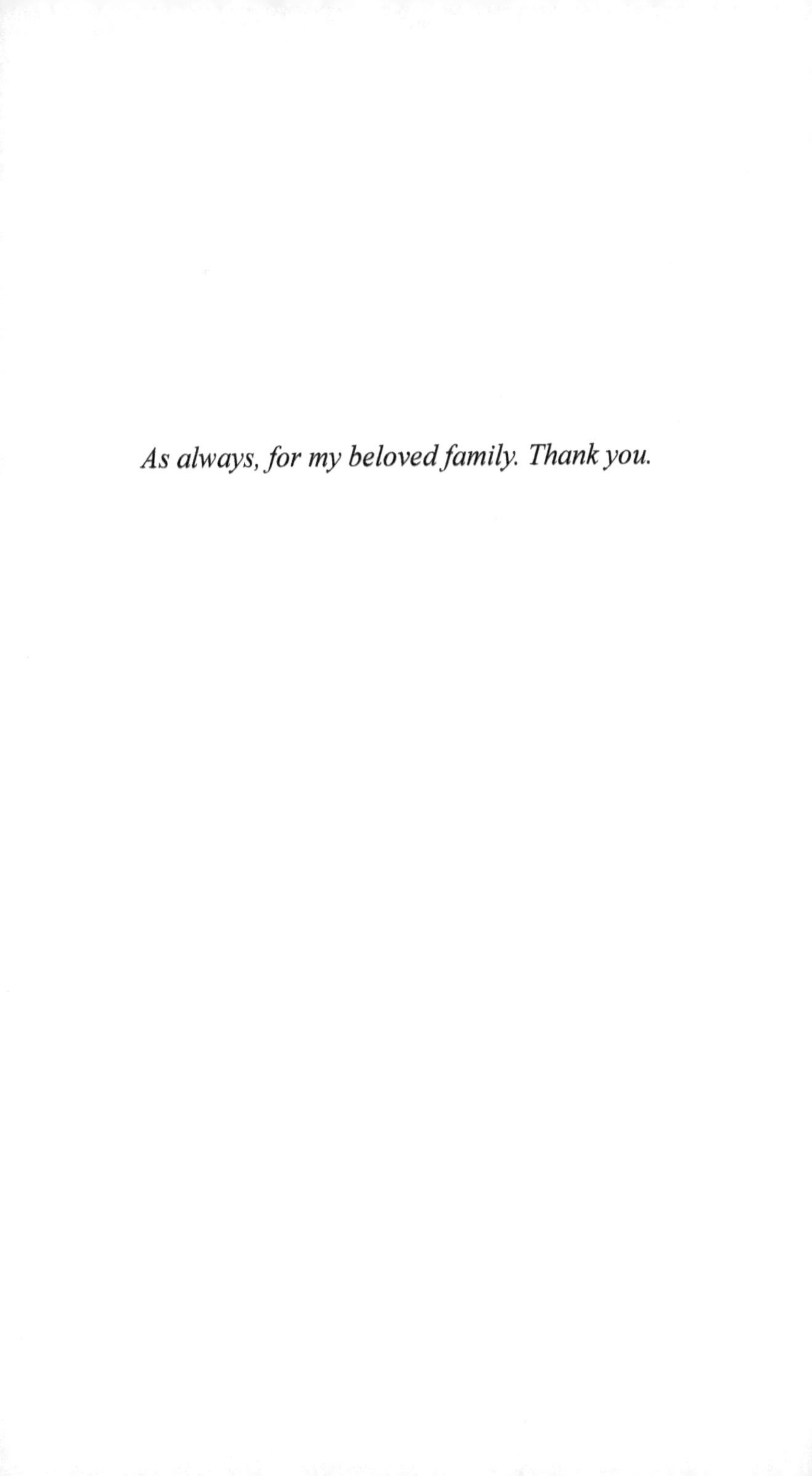

As always, for my beloved family. Thank you.

ONE

Myra contemplated all the mistakes that had led her to this moment, staring down the barrel of a gun held by a very angry wizard inside a sealed steel vault. Everything that had led her here. Not every*thing*. Every*one*. One someone. One mistake.

One big, huge, fucking mistake.

A mistake she'd have to deal with later because now she had to prevent a panicking wizard from shooting her. Which was going to be complicated by the fact that they were both sealed inside this vault, and at any moment, they'd be discovered by shapeshifters. Who would be equally as upset to find Myra and the wizard inside the vault as Myra and the wizard were to *be* in the vault. And since those shifters had a problem with the wizard, and the wizard had a gun —currently pointed at Myra—none of this was good.

She didn't even have a convenient roof to leap off of to save herself. So irritating.

"You did this," the wizard hissed. "You did this on purpose."

"Get sealed inside a vault? You think I arranged *this*? To what end?" She wanted to search the area around the door, see if there was anything she could tweak to get the door opened again. But she couldn't move because gun in her face and angry wizard trapped with her.

"So they'd catch me. This was all a ruse. You're working with the shifters, aren't you?"

Not the ones he was referring to, but that was a technicality that could get her shot. "No. I am not working with these shifters." Absolutely true fact. "I would very much like to not get caught inside this vault by them. Or anyone for that matter. But I can't figure a way out of this while you're pointing a gun at my face."

"How can you get us out? We are *locked inside an impenetrable vault*."

"Yes. I am aware. But impenetrable is… Maybe not the right word here. Let's just call impenetrable a suggestion." At least to her. She had managed to break into some of the most impenetrable places in the city and its surroundings. That's what she did.

Also one of the things that had led to this mess. She'd never regretted that bet to break into the dragon king's hoard more than she did in this moment.

"What does that mean?" the wizard snapped. "A suggestion? No one can get out. We're trapped. If they find us, we're dead. If they don't find us, we'll suffocate. We're dead, one way or the other. If I shoot you, I can blame you. Someone might hear the sound and come get me out. And at the very least, I'll have more oxygen while I hope someone gets me out."

"But you'll be stuck in a tight space with a dead body. Not fun. Trust me. And anyway, if you shoot me, you have no hope of getting out of here without getting caught. I'm good at getting out without getting caught."

"You're caught now. I'd say you suck at it."

"*I'm* not the one who tripped the backup alarm that sealed the door shut." Though, she should have been watching this asshole closer to make sure he didn't trip that alarm.

She still wasn't entirely sure what had happened, how it had happened. She'd had her back to him for all of forty seconds. Next thing she knew they were both staring at the vault door as it slammed shut. And honestly, she'd had no idea a door that big and thick could swing shut that fast. It had taken a hefty heave to get it open once she'd unlocked it. Taken her and the wizard to move the huge round door to one side.

The instant the wizard—his name was Glen. A wizard named Glen. Instead of Astrid or Angelino or something. That felt strange to her— the instant Glen had triggered the backup sensors, Myra had taken one step toward the door, thinking she had time to keep it from sealing. Or at the very least, slip out before the three foot thick ode to engineering closed. She'd have been able to get it to open again from the outside. Maybe a little trickier. It was designed to seal in thieves until the authorities arrived. But she could do it. Wouldn't have been the first time either.

But then the door swung shut too fast for her to get out. So fast, if she'd tried, she'd have been flattened. Squashed dead between the door and the steel frame. Not an end she was excited about.

She didn't particularly want to be shot either.

"Listen," she said with as much patience as she could muster. "I need to examine the door. I might be able to tweak something. But I can't even attempt that while you're pointing a gun at me. So we need a little truce." She shrugged.

"Think of it this way. You can always shoot me later."

That thought obviously mollified him because, though he narrowed his already narrow dark eyes at her, he did lower the gun. Without the gun raised, Glen was a much less intimidating man. Wizards could be that way. Almost innocuous. Very ordinary and human looking. You couldn't just look at someone and assume they were a wizard—wizard was a gender-neutral term despite *some* people's insistence a wizard had to be a man. She'd met wizards who were women, who were nonbinary, who were transgendered, who were gender fluid. Gender had nothing to do with wizard magic. The term wizard applied to the *type* of magic someone wielded.

For example, she would never be referred to as a wizard because she didn't wield wizard magic. She had a different kind of magic. The kind that made breaking-and-entering a very successful career choice.

Glen, on the other hand, had a pretty decent amount of specifically wizard magic inside that wiry body. But it wasn't obvious.

He was taller than her, which wasn't hard, but not a giant. He was razor thin, even a little emaciated in his face, with sharp cheekbones and a narrow nose on which perched small, round, purely decorative glasses. In the right circumstances, he could have graced catwalks because he had that sort of haunted, interesting quality to his face. Not handsome. His eyes were too close together and his jaw too pronounced for handsome. But interesting enough she could see some designers wanting to drape him in their clothing.

He'd tied his long blond hair back into a low tail. And he'd dressed in black trousers and turtleneck for their heist, which was both a bit clichéd but also practical. She was wearing all black, too.

Not that the dark colors were going to save them inside a vault lit up so brightly she'd had to blink a few times when walking through the door.

While the interior of the vault was shockingly scentless, so without scent as to be noticeable even to her when she'd stepped inside, the stench of Glen's stress sweat was starting to permeate the air. That level of panic wasn't good for either of them. But at least he wasn't pointing a gun at her anymore.

"Don't try anything funny," he said, taking a step away from her. "I can shoot you before you can get the gun from me."

"I don't like guns anyway."

She really didn't. And never used them unless

absolutely necessary. In her line of work, it was almost never necessary. Guns were messy and made noise and drew attention. All the opposite of what she did or wanted to do when working.

Once she was sure Glen wasn't going to shoot her the moment she moved, she eased up to the vault door.

The interior of the vault wasn't huge. It was maybe eight by ten feet, lined with security deposit boxes, most of which were just filled with people's wills and family treasures—things like thumb drives with pictures and backup files. Very few would contain anything worth stealing for a thief and a wizard.

One of the boxes, however…

The reason the vault door was impenetrable was because all the family treasures and wills and miscellany belonged to shifters. This wasn't an ordinary security vault. It wasn't on the property of a bank, like human security deposit boxes.

This vault occupied space at the back of a law firms' offices in a mid-rise building in Midtown. A building that blended seamlessly with its neighbors, a couple of high and mid-rise, glass fronted buildings that held office space mostly. The building next to this one had offices on the lower levels and a hotel on the upper floors. Two different elevators. Not that she'd cased that building before.

Okay, she'd cased that building before. But that was just a coincidence. And had nothing to do with her current job. She'd cased a lot of the buildings in this city at one time or another. She was a busy thief.

The building with the law firm's offices was shorter than its neighbors by a few stories, but not enough to look awkward. The front was covered in dark brown, almost black glass, that reflected whatever sunlight got down the tunnel of the Midtown street. There was a coffee shop on the ground floor, and mostly lawyers and accountants in the upper floors, though one level was taken over by a budding new fashion designer's business.

She'd been tempted to sneak in there, just to see what the designer had for next season. Myra wasn't very into fashion for herself personally, but she liked the accessories that went with fashion and tended to keep up on the scene as a sort of side hobby, so she'd know what rich people were into at any given point.

The law firm with the vault was outwardly like any other firm in the building. Except that it was run by Shifters for Shifters—the non-dragon shifters. Dragon shifters had...other avenues of dealing with legal matters. But the average shifter in the city couldn't take advantage of dragon resources and had to do their own thing. The city tolerated shifters and wizards because they had little choice. Especially when the dragon king lived here. But that didn't mean they had to look out for the shifters.

This law firm, one Janu Peters and Schlotz, had an entire floor in the building to itself, and offered this vault for their clients' most prized possessions, because traditional banks could be bigoted toward shifters if they realized a shifter was a shifter. There were laws of course—that's why Janu Peters and Scholtz were in official business—but laws weren't always *helpful* in the ways one might think.

So she was currently trapped in a space full of things a shifter would love, inside a vault designed to withstand shifter strength—even dragon shifter strength—and to block most wizard magic. Wizards and shifters had a very mixed-bag sort of relationship. They either worked together well— with "well" being a subjective term because when they did work together that usually spelled disaster for other people—or they were enemies. There was very little in the way of neutral ground between them. Allies or enemies. No indifferent acquaintances. Ever.

In this case, she was dealing with a wizard whose relationship to shifters was…unknown. That made their position, trapped inside a shifter vault, particularly dicey.

She shouldn't have taken this job. She should have refused. She'd walked into the sort of job she *knew* better than to take.

But when the dragon king asks, it's so hard to say no.

Especially when you have a crush on, possible a budding relationship with, the dragon king's son.

Though, if Christopher knew where she was right now, and that she was here because of his father, he'd be so pissed.

She was pretty ticked off herself, to be honest. But that anger had to wait for later.

First, she had to find a way to crack open a vault from *inside*.

She'd never had to break out of a vault before. Usually, she was breaking into them.

Two

Then

Myra had never driven into the dragon king's compound before. The first time, she'd taken a subway to a nearby station, then hiked up the steep hills to the base of the compound, where she had found a way to sneak into the hoard undetected. At least, undetected long enough to get inside and wander around before someone caught her.

Mistake number one. Taking the bet that she could break into the king's hoard.

Mistake number two. Getting caught.

The other times she'd come to the compound, she'd been flown in. But only by one dragon shifter. Christopher. The thought of letting another dragon shifter carry her the way Christopher did gave her the icks. It felt… Weirdly, it would feel like cheating. Not the sort of cheating she might do at cards. Not the sort of cheating that she occasional felt when using her magic to break into things. She did like old school breaking-and-entering to ensure her skills were up to scratch.

This sort of cheating was the type that had more to do with private relationships and romance. Which…

Well, that part of things between her and Christopher was still delicate. Not quite settled. There was potential there. A tension that was almost as fun as it was spooky. Thinking about Christopher gave her a fluttery feeling in her stomach and being around him gave her tingles and she was pretty eager to explore those tingles with him. But also…

Still hesitating. Still uncertain.

He was the dragon king's son.

And the dragon king was a huge complication to… To everything.

Because of this thing with Christopher that she couldn't label yet, the idea of another dragon shifter holding her in his arms and flying her around the place felt disloyal to Christopher. Like cheating.

She had no idea if the dragons would have viewed it that way. As she'd understood things, the only way in to the mansion was to be flown in. Someone went to the front entrance, they never got past the gates. But instead of sending a dragon to fly her in, or sending Christopher to get her, the way he usually did, this time the dragon king had sent a car for her. A big, long, shiny black limo. She'd never ridden in a limo legitimately before. Snuck into them. Driven them when pretending to be a chauffeur. Hidden in the trunk to sneak in somewhere. Yes.

Invited into the backseat and driven around like she belonged in the car? No.

Driving into the compound gave her a completely different perspective on the place. It was huge when looking at it from above, spread out over the hills on the upper tip of Manhattan. Surrounded by forest. Looking like an ancient castle. The white and golden sandstone walls reinforced by modern steel. Some flat rooftop spaces, which Myra realized while flying in with Christopher were designed to allow airborne dragons a place to land since the surrounding trees did not making a dragon-landing easy. Also, those few flat spaces made for good defense against any potential attacking dragons.

Except for those flat roofs, the main mansion

did look very much like a human palace or castle from the air.

Inside, though, the proportions were odd, better suited to beings that weren't entirely human. Strangely large corridors with ceilings twice as tall as ordinary. Long spaces, double-sized doors, no tight corners or small rooms.

Entering from the ground level, driving in through thick metal gates that rolled back only after the car was scanned by a device set into the wall over the gate, the weird proportions of everything were more obvious. The gate was wide and tall, set into a stone arch in a curtain wall that was topped by spikes. And, she knew from researching to break into the hoard, those spikes weren't just decorative or to prevent pigeons from landing on the wall. They were sharpened, set very close together, and tipped in poison. The kind of poison that a tiny scratch resulted in death.

Climbing the wall and trying to get around the spikes was not a good option for breaking in.

Once through the gates, the drive up to the main building wound through the thick forest, trees crowding the road and making the long limo feel awkward. She kept expecting it to scrape against a branch, kept wondering why the king used a car this long on these tight bends when something smaller would make the switchback turns easier.

Still, the limo made it up the hill and didn't once scrape against a random tree branch or tip out over the top of a gapping drop. Which was pretty impressive.

"Nice driving," she said to her chauffeur, who hadn't spoken the entire time.

He did not disappoint by speaking now. Just held the back door open for her as she climbed out.

She respected that level of commitment to the job.

Looking up at the main, ground-level entrance to the mansion was yet another reminder of the odd proportions. The front door was a double wooden door that looked both wide and tall enough to allow in a big rig truck. Reinforced by steel beams, looking like something from a medieval castle, but with a remarkably ordinary set of modern doorknobs on each door. Brass, ordinary size for human hands, round. The knobs were at the level of her head instead of anywhere a human might have put them, but otherwise, pretty ordinary doorknobs.

The chauffeur pushed one of the two doors open, swinging it inward with what looked like a pretty significant heave of muscle, and let her proceed him inside. She expected him to follow and continue leading her to the king.

Instead, the door closed behind her and she was left standing in a large foyer decorated in dark woods and a brass chandelier hanging from the too high ceiling. This foyer had a different aesthetic to the parts of the mansion she'd seen on prior visits. It was more in keeping with the impression of a medieval castle, right down to the tapestries covering white stone walls.

Myra didn't have a great sense of smell, but the compound smelled strongly of that elusive scent of dragon that was hard to define. Bit dry and reptilian. But also musky, like a mammal. A touch of leather. And with just a hint, very faint and hard to detect on its own, of sulfur.

She couldn't explain it and didn't have a sensitive enough sense of smell to describe it. But it was very distinctly dragon shifter. If there were real dragons in the world still flying around—they were supposedly mostly asleep—Myra imagined they'd smell like this, too.

She stood in the huge foyer wondering why she'd been left alone to wander around, since the first time she'd been here, she'd broken into the king's hoard. Then movement in the shadows of a set of wooden pillars against one wall. The pillars were decorative, as far as she could tell. But maybe not. Because suddenly she was standing in the foyer with someone who hadn't been there a moment ago.

It took her brain a full beat before she realized she was looking at the dragon king himself.

She'd seen him multiple times at this stage, both here and out in the city. The familial resemblance to Christopher was obvious. While the king wasn't quite as tall as his son, he was no slouch in the height department. The angles and planes of his face spoke a similar story to Christopher's. But where Christopher wasn't what one would call conventionally handsome—she thought of him as compelling—the king defined the term.

His dark hair was peppered with silver. His eyes were a changeable blue or green depending on the lighting, with creases around the edges. The first time they'd met, he'd called Christopher a youngling and Myra had assumed she was going to steal a kid back from his kidnappers. Christopher was no a kid. But the fact that his father still spoke of him that way had either been a manipulative lie or the king was just that old and considered Christopher a child still.

Hard to say with the king. Because manipulation and lying were part of his DNA.

"Clever trick, finding me," she said by way of greeting.

"My son isn't the only one who is…intrigued by your movements. And yet neither of us know where you sleep."

She shrugged. "Woman's got to have some secrets. I hope you didn't bring me here to hit on me."

The king tucked his chin, flashing her a sardonic look that was frankly insulting. But also understandable. He was a king. She was a nobody. She liked being a nobody. She did better at her work being a nobody. She'd gone to a lot of trouble cultivating a life of being a nobody to anybody who might be looking. Having a crush on the king's son was bad enough for that nobody status.

She did wonder how both of them kept finding her when she wasn't in her hidey hole, though. Well, Christopher always found her. This was the first time the king had sent someone other than Christopher to get her. Which meant the king was also keeping tabs on her.

Which was *very* inconvenient.

"I require your services again," the king said.

"But you didn't send Christopher to find me."

"That is becoming… A problem."

"A problem, huh? I suppose you're going to tell me how it's a problem. Whether I care or not."

His mouth twitched, and then he smiled fully. "You're clever and sneaky and capable. I do like that about you. I do not like that my son likes you."

More insults. She supposed this wasn't completely unexpected, but somehow, she was still taken by surprise by the turn in this conversation. She honestly hadn't thought the king cared about his son's romantic life enough to bring it up.

"He's the son of a king," the king said, as if reading her mind. "I have…plans."

"Does he know about these plans? Might want to clue him in."

"The time isn't right."

"Gonna have to get it right soon, then. But I'm not sure what any of that has to do with me."

"My son likes you."

She chuckled. "I've read Page Six. Christopher has *liked* a lot of humans over the years." Though, she hadn't known any of that before meeting him. She'd done a crash course in learning all about this particular son of the dragon king after meeting him. And discovered a lot of rumors and innuendo and assumptions and speculation.

And not an awful lot of real information.

That had done more to pique her interest than put her off. She loved a good puzzle.

And a dragon shifter with a soft spot for damsels in distress who also happened to be the son of the dragon king was a definite puzzle.

She narrowed her eyes at the king. "Do you chase away everyone he sees?"

She was going to say dates, but in truth, they'd only been on one date so far, and that had been to one of his apartments to watch a movie. Nothing else had happened that night. She'd fallen asleep. Found herself waking up alone in a scrumptious bed with a note that told her to eat anything she liked and that he'd enjoyed the movie even if she'd fallen asleep.

He hadn't been anywhere in the apartment when she'd gone exploring, and she had to commend him his bravery leaving her alone with all his stuff. She hadn't stolen anything. But she had snooped. That had been a fun few hours, actually.

Still. What was happening between her and Christopher couldn't be called much yet. There was chemistry. There was intent. But there were also nerves and hesitation—mostly on her part. So the king making an issue of it already was strange. Unless he did this all the time.

She idly wondered how the prince Christopher had once dated dealt with this level of interference.

"My youngest does a very good job of chasing off most of his paramours himself," the king said.

"Rude. Does he know you talk about him this way?"

"It's not an insult. He has never gotten serious about any of his past lovers and does all the work of leaving when things get serious. I do not have to interfere."

She couldn't tell what the king was getting at. Was he warning her that Christopher was a short term thing and not to pin her hopes on more? Because she'd have to have hope for more for that to be necessary, and honestly, she didn't know what she wanted or hoped for yet. She liked Christopher. A lot. She wouldn't mind taking him to bed. But beyond that…

"Is this the entire reason I'm here?" she asked. "So you can warn me away from your son for… reasons. Because I do have better things to do." Like plan her next heist. There were many many rich people in the world with too much stuff, and she liked to redistribute that stuff. Or just prove she could swipe it before giving it back. Depended on the rich person.

"As I said, I have a job for you."

"Why don't we get to that, then." She didn't want to do another job for the king, but letting him tell her about it was better than discussing Christopher with him.

Anything was better than listening to the king trying to dissuade her from a relationship with his son.

THREE

Now

The vault door was a solid block of steel, three feet thick and secured into the surrounding brick wall by twelve thick steel pipes. There was a spell on the outside designed to keep wizards from just bespelling the lock open—which honestly most wizards couldn't do. That was a her-skill, not a wizard-skill. But the spell also seemed to block wizard's magic inside the vault too.

Which was why Myra's jumpy wizard accomplice had a gun.

She really disliked working with people who carried guns. So messy. So much room for disaster.

Already a disaster since they were locked inside a vault.

Maybe she should have encouraged the king to keep discussing all the reasons she shouldn't see his son.

From outside, she'd been able to finagle the code lock and had a spell that worked on the paw-print screen, disguising her ordinary human hand as a wolf-shifter paw. Fortunately, the paw print requirement wasn't specific to any one wolf-shifter. That would have made things much more difficult. She suspected that was an oversight by the lock designers. Or else no one knew how to program biometrics to more than a general shape for a shifter's print. Since she hadn't encountered a biometrics paw scan that was specific to individual shifters yet, maybe the techs hadn't figured that out yet.

Even the dragon king hadn't had a specific hand print biometric lock on his hoard. The eye scan had been interesting, since it *was* specific to a dragon's eye…

She shook off the thoughts for later research. She'd only started working more around shifters and wizards—usually she avoided both as much as possible and stuck to breaking-and-entering human facilities and houses and such—so some of the finer details hadn't crossed her work situations before.

In fact, she hadn't even known all that much about dragon shifters until that unfortunate breaking-into-the-king's-hoard incident. Since then, because of Christopher mostly, she'd really been trying to learn more about dragon shifters. And hadn't *that* been eye-opening research.

These weren't dragon shifters, though. Most of the lawyers and two of the three firm partners were wolf-shifters. So the paw print being wolf-shifter made sense. And, again fortunately, the shifters hadn't considered blocking *her* kind of magic. Just wizard magic. She had a feeling shifters and wizards knew as little about her magic, the specifics of it at least, as she'd known about dragon shifters.

That had made breaking into the vault a lot easier. But the breaking out part...

The blocks on magic inside the vault were a lot stronger than the ones on the outside. Maybe those increased once the interior alarm had been triggered. She hadn't tried to use any of her thief magic inside the vault before the alarm and the door sealing shut again. She hadn't actually had much time to do anything but look for the specific security box they needed. She hadn't even attempted to open that box yet when the door closed.

Now, she realized that the blocks inside the vault were doing a number on her magic, not just Glen's. When she tried to sense her way into the lock from this side, she came up against a blank wall. That was not normal. A touch and she could usually "read" a lock. Even if she used more traditional methods to crack it—which she often did, especially if the lock was challenging—she could get a read on the type of lock it was and how best to get through it.

She could usually sense a magic trap on a lock as well, which had saved her tripping an alarm more than once. Spells on locks weren't uncommon. Even humans bought those. So she tended to check automatically.

With the inner vault door, though, she couldn't sense the lock, couldn't pick up any spells. Actually felt a lot of blankness when she tried to use a small spell to even reveal the locking mechanism. Nothing.

Her magic was officially useless inside the vault.

Shit.

She could do this the old-fashioned way. Maybe. But as she'd never had to break *out* of a vault before, she wasn't sure what the old-fashioned way was because she couldn't even see the locking mechanism.

She cursed in her head again, but rolled her lips into her mouth so she didn't curse out loud. Her companion was jumpy enough as is.

Okay, so. She couldn't get at the door locks from this side. Yet. Maybe there was something else in here that would help. Or maybe she could find the spell that was blocking her magic. If it wasn't baked into the vault walls—in which case she'd be well and truly fucked—then it would have to be set into something, a device of some kind. That's how this kind of thing had to work. Couldn't just have a spell floating in the air. It had to have an anchor. Otherwise, it dissipated. If that anchor was something she could find—and not the vault walls—maybe she could dismantle the spell.

Did they have time for that?

No one had opened the vault yet, so hopefully. Not that she'd mind the vault door being opened. She'd rather face the shifters than slowly die of asphyxiation in a room with a wizard holding a gun, who might shoot her to conserve the oxygen. But having time to break out of the vault without anyone being the wiser would be better.

She started a methodical search, checking the walls, hovering a hand over the various deposit box doors. When she reached the door of the box they'd been sent for, she hovered a beat longer. But not too long. She expected the wizard to say something, to say they should get what they were there for and then worry about getting out. But he didn't comment.

Maybe he didn't want to get caught holding incriminating evidence if the shifters found them before they could escape.

What was that called? Plausible deniability. He could make up any kind of story to get out of this if caught, but not if he was holding something he wasn't supposed to be holding.

Still, she was surprised he didn't mention anything about the box when she paused at it. Not even a suggestion they look inside and make sure what they'd come for was even there. She was tempted by that logic herself. But she wanted a way out first. *Then* she could get on with the theft part of her night.

She didn't sense anything from the specific box that was any stronger or more pronounced than any other box. They all felt like blank slates to her. Black holes of nothingness. The fact that the box they were aiming for was just as blank and protected in the exact same way as the other boxes, some of which held nothing more than pictures and wills and maybe a few family heirlooms, was interesting.

Because either the law firm applied the same security to all their boxes, no matter the content, or the contents of the box she was here for were not what she'd been told.

And wouldn't that just be a kick in the pants.

She hated working for the dragon king.

She missed Christopher.

That last thought was incredibly scary, though, so she pushed it aside. Better to be angry with the father than to dwell on her softer feelings for the son. She got soft, she was going to get killed. Or worse…

Have her entire life taken over by the dragon king.

That was starting to happen already. And she hated it. But again, a problem to deal with when—*if*—she got out of this vault.

The search of the boxes turned up nothing specific. She glanced at the vault door again. No hint that someone was outside waiting to get in. She scanned the vault for a camera, something recording them, but couldn't see any obvious signs of one. Didn't mean there wasn't one, just that if there was, it was well disguised.

She hunted around the base of the walls, near the floor. The room was a steel case reinforced by brick, reinforced by titanium in the outer layer. Again, designed to prevent shifters from breaking in, and some of those shifters had the kind of strength that made pulling a traditional vault out of a brick wall possible. The extra layer of titanium *outside* the brick and steel exterior of the vault was the real kicker.

When nothing suspicious or useful turned up around the baseboards, she searched high, near the ceiling. At first from the floor. Then she brought out some of her climbing suction cups from her multi-pocket vest that she went nowhere without, and climbed up the two it took her to reach high enough she could study the line where wall met ceiling.

The wizard watched all this with a scowl, his gun lowered but his finger hovering too close to the trigger along the barrel. At least he wasn't stupid enough to stand around with his finger on the trigger. One loud noise and he'd shoot his foot off, and then she'd have to deal with that. Blood was messy and obvious. Hard to explain away blood.

She hit a corner of the vault, studying the spot where all the angles came together, and finally spotted a camera or recording device of some kind. A tiny device, very advanced, with an illusion spell to keep it disguised. It was little more than the size of one of those button batteries, easy to overlook even without the illusion spell.

The spell itself was pretty simple. Anchored to the camera, but not designed to stand up to close scrutiny. Just to hide from casual observers.

And now her face was in it. Which meant somewhere, someone had a recording of her face, close up. That wasn't great news, but she could mitigate that issue. She touched a finger to the little camera. Studied the spells around it.

The realization hit her a moment later—longer than it should have taken her to realize—that the illusion spell was working up here, when other magic inside the vault was dampened. And she could sense the illusion spell. And study the camera with a touch.

Her magic worked up here.

She glanced down the few feet below her to where Glen was silently glaring up at her.

The minute she made eye contact, he said, "What did you find?"

"Camera."

She dislodged the button, taking the illusion spell with it, and hopped off the suction cups she'd been using as toe and finger holds while she studied the ceiling. Because of the magic dampening in the vault, she'd had to manually move those suction cups around to study different locations. That was less efficient. Also a bit irritating.

Once she was back to floor level, the illusion spell on the button camera broke. She felt it break. Not just dissipate or stop working. It actually *broke*, like thin glass shattering, the shards falling to the floor. That left the camera exposed, an obvious circle of silver on her fingertip. But also revealed something about the way the magic dampening effects worked inside the vault. Any spell she'd come into the vault with, anything *active* she'd brought inside the vault with her, would have broken the instant she was inside.

Interesting.

Now she was even more determined to find the source of the spell. And maybe take it with her so she could study the spell at her leisure.

So long as she could get out of the vault of course.

FOUR

Then

The dragon king led Myra through a series of corridors she hadn't seen before, keeping her in suspense about his reasons for bringing her here, and the job he wanted to hire her to do, because he was a drama king as well as a dragon king. She should have expected the suspense.

The conversation about her relationship with Christopher still had her reeling though. Off balance. Because her relationship with Christopher, whatever it was and was developing into, also had her off balance and reeling a bit. She wasn't prepared to discuss this with his *father*. That his father didn't like the relationship, whatever it was, didn't bode well. But also, it was none of the dragon king's business. And she was just obstinate enough to want to see Christopher just to annoy the king.

Except…

She didn't want her…whatever was happening with Christopher to be something she got involved in just to irritate the king. She *liked* Christopher. She wanted what was developing between them to be between them. With no irritating, domineering third party having any influence or say over the matter.

The corridors through the palace were remarkably empty. They usually were when she was here with Christopher, too. The occasional shifter in human form passing, but most of the time, just empty hallways with weird proportions —very high ceilings and oddly wide walls, but in a way that almost felt narrow. The wooden floors gave way to marble floors in a few hallways, then returned to wood.

The walls in one corridor were decorated with huge hanging pictures of dragons, and landscapes, and the occasional battle scene—she'd have liked to study those closer because she suspected they had hints of actual dragon history in them, but the king didn't let her linger. In other corridors, the walls were hung with tapestries, or displayed ancient weaponry in display cases. And in one notable corridor, the white walls were as empty and blank as the black marble floors. That was one of the most disorienting corridors because it felt so blank, like it was half finished and awaiting the final details.

The underlying dragon smell permeated all of it. No matter where they went, that collective smell of dragon lingered in the air. She was a little surprised by how pleasant the scent of dragon shifters was, even with the very faint hint of brimstone at the base. That was probably down to how she felt about Christopher, though, and that she associated that smell with him. Well that and the smell of sugar cookies. That Christopher sometimes smelled like her favorite cookie amused her.

Finally, after what felt like a purposefully long walk to show off his mansion—to a thief!—the king led her into small conference room. Small being a relative word. The room still had inordinately high ceilings. But it was more roughly human-sized otherwise, like a boardroom in a Manhattan office building. Dark blue carpets covered the floor, the walls were wood paneled on three sides and a bank of floor to ceiling windows made up the fourth wall. The windows looked out over the forest, down into the valley below the hill the mansion sat on. Beyond the hill, she could just see the rising cityscape of Manhattan. She thought of that as "below" them since it was heading downtown. But also, given the king's compound was up on a hill, there was the illusion of the city being "below" the king's perch.

The center of the room was taken up by a large wooden conference table surrounded by cushiony black desk chairs. A rectangular device in the center of the conference table probably controlled audio-visual equipment, but she didn't see any screens or TVs or anything to display charts and graphs. Her experience with conference rooms was usually confined to creeping through them in the dark on her way to steal something, though, so maybe the screen or TVs were hidden.

She didn't see any closets or hidden panels at first glance, but after wandering to the windows to pretend to take in the views, she spotted the hidden panel in the wall to the left and the subtle cameras placed in the four corners of the room.

"Nice." She turned to face the king.

He was also looking out the window and he nodded briefly at her comment so he'd made the assumption she'd wanted him to—that she'd been talking about the view.

"We attending a board meeting or something?" She gestured to the table.

"I need you to retrieve a necklace from a vault," the king said abruptly.

Okay. So. Right to the point. She was good with that. This tour of the mansion felt like stalling and she didn't like stalling when she wasn't the one doing it.

"What sort of necklace, and why, and why haven't you just bought it?" She'd seen his hoard, probably one of the few humans to have, and she knew it wasn't just random piles of gold and free gemstones. There were plenty of necklaces and piles of jewelry. "What makes this necklace special enough you need it stolen?"

"It's not for sale," he answered the most obvious question. "It's magical." Which sort of explained why it was special, but the king also had other magical necklaces. "And it is dangerous."

"How so?"

"It's held in a vault guarded by shifters."

"It's not like that amulet you already have, right?" The amulet the shifters who'd kidnapped Christopher had wanted in exchange for Christopher's return. An amulet that would essentially turn shifters into monsters. Bad bad bad. If this was something like that, then yes, it was dangerous.

"No. Not precisely." The king let his gaze travel over the room as he said that.

He thought he was subtle, and a good actor. And he actually did do a good job of being himself in public in a loud and obviously bombastic way. He was also good at court machinations, according to Christopher, which were all about deceit and hiding motivations. So she wasn't entirely sure if that refusal to make eye contact meant he was really hiding something or he was attempting to make her think he was hiding something. Either way, he was attempting to intrigue her. Which was the way to get her to take a job she didn't necessarily want to take.

If she'd been a shifter, she'd probably have been a cat shifter of some sort, and then along with the usual cat burglar jokes, she'd also have to deal with her mental "curiosity killed the cat" jokes because her curiosity was definitely an issue. Also, that subtle sense of challenge got to her.

The king was entirely too skilled at manipulation and she was afraid he had her number.

"Where's the vault?"

"Midtown building. Lawyers' office suite."

"Not a bank?"

"These lawyers specialize in handling shifter cases. It can be hard for a shifter to get good and fair representation among human lawyers." He sneered the word human.

She tried not to take offense, even if he meant to give offense. "Not sure why that means they need a whole vault in their offices and not one inside a bank." But that didn't matter much to the job. "Why is it better for you to have this necklace rather than it staying nice and safe and unused inside a vault?"

"The necklace is dangerous and there are others after it," the king said. "It will be safer inside my hoard."

She'd heard that story before. But in this case, she suspected "safer" meant "I'll have it and no one else will" because in the grand scheme of things, the king was still a dragon who hoarded valuable things for the sake of hoarding valuable things.

"Why not just negotiate that with the lawyers, then?" A test of sorts in that question. "Why steal the necklace? Why not buy it."

"As I already said, it's not for sale."

"But if it's dangerous, and your hoard is really the safest place for it, wouldn't the owners *want* it to be safer?"

"The owners do not realize the necklace's potential."

Of course not. "And you do?"

"I have been fully briefed on the situation."

"By?"

The door to the conference room opened again and a new man walked into the room. Tallish, though not as tall as the king, very thin, high cheekbones, dark eyes, long blond hair hanging loosely around his shoulders. He wore a business suit in a dark charcoal gray with a white shirt and purple tie. A pair of tiny round glasses perched on his nose, glasses she could tell at a glance were for effect rather than necessity, and he kept his hands clasped in front of him.

He looked innocuous, very human, and probably the sort of person no one would look at too closely.

She pegged him immediately as a wizard.

FIVE

Now

Glen leaned in close to Myra's finger and pointed at the silver button she held on the tip. "That doesn't look like a camera."

This close, Glen's nervous sweat stink was a bit stronger. The man was seriously stressed. If she could smell him, with her not great sense of smell, things were bad. If the shifters caught them now, they'd probably be hit in the face with that sign of his fear.

"It's called a button camera and mostly it's a short distance device for recording. It will be motion activated, which means it turned on the minute we got inside the vault, and the recording it's making is probably nearby in a security room or security closet."

"How do you know that?" Glen barked, glaring at her.

She ignored the glare, frowning as she glanced around the vault interior again. "Part of the job to know these things. Standard operating procedure. The button doesn't have a strong signal. The recorder would have to be close."

Outside of the camera, even searching baseboards and ceiling, she hadn't found the magic dampening device. There weren't a lot of hiding places inside the vault. It wasn't that large. And any spells in spots lower than the ceiling would have broken so there wasn't anything being hidden by an illusion.

She hadn't been able to sense anything from the safety deposit boxes lining the walls. But those were the only option for hiding the magic dampening device. She glanced at the locked vault door, still decidedly sealed against exit. No one busting in to stop them or catch them or kill them. But would they allow her time to search all the deposit boxes?

Maybe they didn't think she could open them.

Magically breaking locks was far from her only skill. And she liked doing things the old-fashioned way. Testing her abilities. Seeing if she was good enough.

Most of the time, she was.

But safety deposit boxes were tricky. They took two different keys. And all the keys were different. This required a bit of technology if she wasn't using magic. Fortunately, she'd brought the technology—a sort of key imprinting and replicating machine—because she'd thought she'd need it for the deposit box that was their goal. She hadn't intended on opening more than the one box, though.

Opening every single box would take all night, maybe a couple of days. She was certain they didn't have that kind of time. The air in the vault would run out. She estimated they had about five more hours of breathable air. Then they were dead.

She planned on being out of this place before that. But she didn't have enough time to search every single security box in the meantime.

Where to start?

She considered the little button camera on her fingertip. Did she smash it or keep it? Smashing it might set off an alarm—though so many had probably sounded by now that hardly seemed something she needed to worry about—and it might bring the shifters sooner rather than later.

That had the benefit of getting them out of the vault sooner, but the drawback of getting them into a different sort of trouble sooner too. And without the prize they'd come for.

If she didn't smash the camera, the shifters would be getting a recording of everything she did. And that could be used against her in a court of law. Which she had no intention of being in. Dealing with the recordings they might already have was an issue she had to see to after they got out. So far, the only thing she could be accused of was breaking into the vault and getting stuck. She hadn't technically stolen anything yet and could plausibly deny being here to steal things if she never tried to open a deposit box.

But she had to open at least a few of the deposit boxes.

So. Smash camera or put it in her pocket. She couldn't tell by looking at it if it was also recording voices. Voice recordings would be as bad as video evidence, or nearly so. She suspected Glen would have a hard time not asking questions, and since he had a gun, he wasn't exactly ignorable.

Okay. She really had little choice. Crush the camera. If someone showed up, they'd be free of the vault. If no one showed up, she'd have time to check for the magic dampening device and hopefully also retrieve the item they were here to get.

She dropped the little camera to the hard linoleum-over-steel-and-concrete floor and smashed the button with the heel of her soft-soled shoes. She felt the stomp reverberate up her calf. Heard a satisfying crunch. She ground her heel down harder into the button, just to make sure. If she'd been wearing harder soled shoes, she'd have known the button was completely shattered with that first stomp, but her shoes had been selected for their ability to limit any sound she made, not crush small electronic devices.

She lifted her foot to see a nice collection of tiny bits of metal and wires flattened into the gray floor. If that thing was still recording, it would be a miracle. Or magic. And the magic couldn't work down here.

Myra glanced at the vault door and held perfectly still for a full three minutes, waiting on signs someone was going to open that door and rush in to arrest them. Or kill them. During that three minutes, she had to shush Glen once. But only once. Which she counted as progress.

He rubbed a hand across his mouth, the gleam of sweat on his upper lip obvious in the vault's mercilessly bright lighting.

At the three minute mark, when it became

obvious no one was rushing in to stop them, she turned her attention to the security boxes. She still wasn't sure where to start looking for the magic dampening device. She had to find that if she had any hope of breaking them out of the vault from the inside. But she hadn't a clue which box to try first.

She did know which box she was here to rob, though.

She decided to start there. She could move on to checking other boxes after. She really didn't want to get caught red handed with the very thing they were here to steal, but she also didn't know where else to start.

From inside one of the many pockets in the black vest she wore over her black yoga pants and black t-shirt, she pulled out the small rectangular device she used for making keys. It was a sort of 3D printer, printing whatever she pressed into the memory foam type substance inside the box.

She needed something for it to copy and print, though, which was where the little tube of super soft, malleable clay-like substance came in. It was stiffer than the foam inside the box, but could be inserted into a lock to form the ridges and contours that would make up the key necessary to open the lock. The substance was nowhere near strong enough to actually open anything. It took the impression of the key, but if she twisted it in an attempt to open the lock, all she'd do is twist the impression and mess the whole thing up.

Carefully, she inserted the tube into one of the two locks keeping the security box sealed. She counted to five, then gently slid the tube back out again, working hard not to flinch or turn it in any way. The impression had to be perfect, or the resulting key would never work, and for that to happen, she couldn't afford to introduce any flaws.

Once out, she examined the impression. Looked clean. She gave the substance a few seconds to harden enough it could be copied. A little warm rub of her fingers and it would soften into the malleable clay-like substance again. But it was just stiff enough after a few seconds to press into the memory foam grid and get an impression that the tiny printer could replicate exactly in a hard plastic.

The hard plastic key would work in the lock.

She went through the procedure twice. Making one of each of the keys necessary to opening the deposit box. Then she returned her little printer to her pocket, and neatly slid the two keys into their respective locks.

When the box clicked open, Glen finally made a noise. A sort of hissing, quiet cheer, like he was trying to keep in a gleeful shout. Myra appreciated his attempt to keep his enthusiasm in check.

"I didn't think you'd be able to pull that off," he murmured.

Why he was whispering, she wasn't sure. The vault was too thick for their voices to carry outside it, and she'd smashed the one camera she'd been able to find. If there were any other listening devices inside the vault, she hadn't found them.

"Trust, Glen. You need to have some faith."

"In a thief?" He snorted.

"Rude. But yes. I'm a very good thief. You should have faith in my ability to steal things."

He didn't comment. Probably for the best.

She slid out the small metal box that occupied the cubby, and swung around to open it while Glen was watching. Last thing she needed was him deciding she'd palmed something to screw him over if what they expected to be inside this box wasn't inside this box.

"Ready?" she asked him.

He nodded, his full attention on the rectangular metal lid. "Open it."

She did.

Six

Then

"The king said the job was to steal a necklace." Myra stared at the wizard, then looked at the dragon king, then glanced back at the wizard. This didn't feel like a good turn of events. And she was definitely not happy about the wizard's presence.

"It's actually a locket, not a full necklace," the wizard, Glen, said. "The locket is the important part." He glanced at the dragon king, but the king kept his attention on Myra. The king hadn't spoken since Glen started explaining the specifics of what they were after.

Myra ignored the king's stare outwardly to keep her attention on the wizard, but she was very aware of his gaze and that focus made her skin itch.

Behind Glen, through the wall of windows at his back, the distant skyline of Manhattan sparkled, sunlight reflecting off the tall, mirror-windowed buildings. At this distance, over the top of a forest, the city looked almost like a fairytale land. And she was in the palace, looking down at it. Except she sat in a very modern boardroom, at a large wooden conference table, across from an actual wizard, with a dragon sitting at the head of the table.

Her life was a little weirder and more fairytale like than she'd prefer. Not like those sanitized-for-kids fairytales either. But like the real fairytales where people cut off their own toes and the fairies sucked poor, unsuspecting humans dry.

Myra repressed a shiver, glad that, as far as she knew, real fairies didn't exist. Dragon shifters and wizards were bad enough.

"It's ancient," Glen continued. "Used to belong to wizards in eons past. But it disappeared. Became more of a myth."

She'd encountered those sorts of relics before. Stolen a few of them over the years. A lot of them ended up in private family collections, passed down with other wealth, and the wealthy people in possession of them usually didn't even know what they had. Which would explain why the king had said the owners of this locket didn't know the locket's potential.

Myra had built a career on stealing those kinds of things. Forgotten things. Things no one realized were missing until too late.

"It's turned up again in the possession of a wolf-shifter family," Glen said of this missing locket. "The locket does not belong to shifters. It's dangerous for shifters to possess it."

She'd heard that story before, too. "Except I understood they didn't know what they had. Or was I misled, and they do know what this locket can do?"

Glen flicked another glance at the king. This time, Myra felt the king's gaze move away from her. She knew without looking when the king's attention landed on Glen because the wizard flinched and looked away quickly.

"They don't know what it is, what it can do," Glen said. "At least, from what I can tell, they don't. They're keeping the locket in a vault inside a law firm. The firm represents shifters who can't find human lawyers who will work with them."

Glen's lip curled just a little, but Myra couldn't tell if he was sneering at the shifters or the humans who didn't want to work with them.

"Since they don't know what they have,"

Myra said, watching Glen closely even as she felt the king's attention move back to the side of her face, "why is it dangerous for them to have this locket? It seems the safest place for something dangerous is locked away in a vault with no one worried about finding it or using it."

Despite the king's assertion the artifact would be safer in his hoard, she wasn't seeing the logic. Leaving something dangerous safely locked away from the world, in the possession of people who weren't going to use it—in this case because they didn't know what they had—was always better than having said dangerous thing out in the world in the possession of people who might use it.

She had no illusions that whatever this locket did, Glen would just lock it away safely and never use it. He wasn't going to all this trouble for nothing.

"The lawyers are suspicious," Glen said. "The ones who have the vault in their office. They know…something. I'm not sure how much. But if they discover the truth, it'll mean bad things for all wizards."

"Do I get to know what these bad things for wizards might be?" she asked, and finally turned her attention on the king. "And what all this has to do with the dragons?"

"I'm merely here as a facilitator," the king

said, his gaze steady on hers. "Glen came to me for help."

Except that the king wanted this necklace-locket in his own hoard and not in Glen's possession. She wondered if Glen knew that part.

"Why? Why would a wizard come to you?"

They both looked at Glen.

"Why come to the dragon king," Myra asked him directly, "another shifter, for help retrieving something you don't want shifters to have?"

Glen did this thing with his shoulders that might have been a shrug. "The king has resources that I don't have access to. Like the name of a good thief."

She didn't wince at that. But she wanted to. This didn't bode well if word had gotten out the king had a thief on the books, ready to do jobs he assigned her. That wouldn't do at all. No. She didn't work for the king. She wasn't one of the king's dragons. And she was not on retainer with him. She worked alone, for herself, and intended on keeping things that way.

She glanced at the king. He blinked slowly at her, but that was his only reaction.

"And I can't go to other wizards," Glen added.

This wasn't entirely unexpected. Wizards working together was a bit like wizards working with shifters. They either did and were tight allies, or they didn't and were basically mortal enemies.

She was starting to believe the problem here was the wizards.

"Why not?" she asked anyway, wondering if she'd get a specific answer or some hand wavey excuse.

She got the hand wavey excuse. "None of them understand the danger. They don't care enough to help me."

Glen was lying. That was interesting.

"But it's important to get the locket back into wizard hands," he finished, his gaze dancing to the king before settling on her again.

She turned to fully face the king. "You think this is important enough to ask me to do the job?"

"I think it's best if this locket is not in possession of the shifter law firm," the king said. Very carefully.

"Whose paying me?" She looked between the two men, swiveling a little in her chair.

Glen did another of those quick glances at the king, then said, "I have some money to pay you. It's not a fortune, but it's something."

She didn't like anything about this. Her hackles were raised. Her suspicions up. Glen had some secret purpose he wasn't discussing. The king had his own agenda in this. And she'd get caught in the middle if she took this job.

A wise thief would say no. She was a wise thief.

But she was also a dangerously curious thief.

"Wire the money to my account by the end of the day. The king has the details. We go in in three days. I'll need the time to research and set up the heist."

Glen blinked hard a few times, opened his mouth, closed it again. Glanced at the king. Faced her again.

She nearly smiled. She liked keeping people on their toes.

"You'll do it? You'll help me?"

"If I can't get into the vault, I'll let you know and refund your money less my research fee." But she was sure she could get into the vault.

"I'm coming with you," Glen said.

She frowned. "No. I don't work with other people."

She ignored the slight eyebrow raise from the king she could sense more than see in her peripheral vision. She knew he was thinking about Christopher. Because she had been working with Christopher lately. But that was unusual. She didn't usual work with other people except as occasional contract labor when she needed help with new tech or a computer hack she couldn't manage on her own.

"I'm going with you. That's part of the deal. I need to be there. I need to…to retrieve the locket myself. I just can't get into the vault on my own."

"Don't trust me to get the locket for you, Glen?" she asked with a small smile. She wouldn't necessarily trust her either if she didn't know her so well.

"It's not that." Glen's gaze once again flicked to the king and back to her. "I need to be there. The locket would be dangerous for you to touch. You'll need a wizard to handle it. You'll need me there."

A jumpy wizard who was telling her any number of lies, might have lied to the king, and whose real motivation in all this was pretty sketchy along for the ride during a break-in.

Yeah, that would turn out well.

But if he was right and the locket needed a wizard to handle it safely, she was going to have to take him along.

She hated working with amateurs.

SEVEN

Now

Inside the security deposit lock box, resting on a small purple silk patch of material, sat the very thing Myra had broken into this vault to steal.

There hadn't been any pictures of the locket when she'd researched it. In fact, there'd been no information on it at all. Glen hadn't really given her enough to find the locket in the histories, and since the shifters didn't know what they had, there weren't any more modern stories about it. She'd come across one single, possible story of a wizard locket that possessed mystical powers to control time. But that was the closest she'd managed to find. And there'd been no descriptions or images of that locket.

So finally getting to see the locket was a moment for pause.

It was round, about half the size of her palm, which made it larger than she'd been expecting, and was made of a greenish polished stone, with swirls of purple and gold color in it like marble. The stone was surrounded by a silver frame, with a pattern of twists and folds in the silver that gave the whole thing movement. It wasn't hanging on a chain of any kind, despite the king having called this a necklace. But there was a little hook of silver at the top where a chain could be strung. There weren't any runes or etchings in the stone's surface or woven into the silver frame. The locket just looked like a pretty, if large, pendant.

"It opens?" she asked Glen with her attention still on the locket. She assumed it did since Glen called it a locket and not a charm or medallion, but she couldn't see a clasp in the silver frame.

"It does. But only for a wizard." Glen reached into the box to retrieve the artifact.

When she looked at his expression, she didn't particularly like what she saw. The gleam in his eyes. The avarice. She'd known this job was hinky from the start. She still wasn't sure if the problem with it all was the king or Glen. Though, given his expression, she was certain Glen was *a* problem now.

She hadn't touched the charm on purpose, because Glen had claimed that would be dangerous. But as she watched him stare wide-eyed at the locket, she did reach in and touch the silk pouch the charm had been resting on, to see if there was anything there she could read. Her magic mostly worked to pick up things like spells and traps set to keep locks secure. She wouldn't be able to just feel wizard magic and know what it was for. Her magic had its limits. But she'd sense a spell or trap if that's what the locket was.

She picked up a few sparks from the silk, but nothing she could clearly identify.

Except... Except she could pick up the magic.

Her magic wasn't being blocked anymore.

Frowning, she hurried back to the vault door and touched the area near the lock. There. She could sense her way into it now. Sense the lines and follow the paths that took her to where she needed to go to get the door open from this side.

Whatever had been dampening magic inside the vault wasn't anymore.

She looked back at Glen. He still held his gun in one hand, but it was pointed at the floor and he seemed unaware that he still held it. His full attention was on the locket. He was smiling, rubbing his thumb over the green polished stone in the center. He murmured a spell under his breath, too quiet for her to catch the words, and the green stone shimmered and seemed to fold backward in a way that wasn't possible for regular stone, revealing an inner chamber, a small depression inside the larger stone.

In the depression, a diamond the size of a corn kernel winked in the overhead florescent lights. Rainbows danced along its surface, reflecting on Glen's tiny round glasses.

Glen's smile grew.

"You can open the door now?" he asked without looking up at her.

"Yeah. You ready to go?"

He nodded. "Oh yeah. I'm ready."

She had no idea what the diamond was—beyond probably worth a tidy sum all on its own—and what the locket really did, but she did want out of this vault sooner rather than later so questions and concerns about the locket could wait.

And since no security had come charging in the minute they opened that box and retrieved the locket, she was starting to suspect no one had been monitoring the vault's camera, or that any alarms had gone off when she'd crushed it under her shoe. There could still be people—security guards or police—on their way. But if they were out there somewhere just beyond the vault door, they'd have probably opened the door by now.

She still had time to get out of this cleanly. Or at least cleanly enough to deal with what dirt was left behind. But she sensed in her little thief soul that her window for escape was closing.

She went to work on the vault lock, using her magic to burrow down into the layers of security. It took her longer from this side, almost a full minute to crack the code. She didn't need the biosensor's paw print this time, though. Probably because, without magic, no one would be able to pick the vault lock from this side of the door.

When the steel bars clicked and clanked out of the wall, sliding into the door, Myra smiled. She gave the big, heavy circle a shove and the door hissed open with a release of air. The fresh air from outside the vault rushed in, brushing the fine hairs that had escaped her bun. She pulled in a deep breath, only then realizing how stale the air inside the vault had been getting.

Wow, they'd had less time than she realized. That would be a terrifying thought later if she chose to dwell on it.

She eased around the door, searching the office beyond.

Empty.

Weird but also she was going to accept the gift horse, as they say, and just get out while the getting was good. They'd even gotten what they'd come for. In the moments after the vault door had closed and locked them in, she'd worried about that part.

"This way," she whispered and motioned Glen to follow her without looking back at him.

She crept forward on noiseless feet, waiting for the telltale sound of running security guards. She reached the office door that moved them into the corridor beyond, and paused again to listen. At one end of the long hallway, an emergency staircase led out of the building. At the other, a private elevator. Offices of various sizes and a couple of conference rooms lined the hall. There was one side corridor that branched off the main one and led to the partners' offices. To the left of the private elevator was a reception desk and small foyer. To the right of the private elevator, a glass door that led out to a bank of public elevators.

The private elevator inside the offices was a pretty unique feature of the building. A security issue, she'd have thought. But where there's money...

Given the law firm often represented shifters pro bono, she was curious where the money came from. Had to be some high profile and wealthy clients in there somewhere.

Which meant she'd probably left at least one security deposit box full of actual valuables back in that vault. Shame.

She eased open the door when she didn't hear anything and studied the corridor. It was dark, with only a set of emergency lights on over the private elevator. Light from the public elevator bank came in through the glass doors, but the rest of the office was dark. Still no signs of security.

They'd set off an alarm, locked themselves in the vault, found and crushed the only camera in the place, and they were still being left alone with no cops arriving to arrest them?

Something about that was…wrong.

Her every instinct hummed. Not that this job had felt right from the beginning. She knew Glen had been lying to her from the start. But the fact that he'd been so willing to shoot her inside the vault, his panic sweat, his visible fear, that would have been hard to fake. She knew he'd panicked. That the vault locking them in wasn't actually part of the plan.

At least, she was pretty sure it hadn't been.

But what she was certain of was that the lack of response to all the alarms they'd triggered was super suspicious. And something was not right.

"Private elevator," Glen said.

That had been her original plan. It was locked down with codes and paw print bio scanners, like the vault, but she could get past those exactly as she had with the vault.

Then she'd be stuck inside another metal box with a jumpy wizard who still had a gun.

"Stairs," she said.

"They'll expect that."

"*They* should already be here to arrest us," she said. "*They* are not working according to plan." Which meant she couldn't make assumptions about what would happen next. The only thing she knew was that she didn't want to be stuck in another metal box with Glen and his gun.

"I'm taking the elevator. That was our plan."

"Help yourself." Their plan had also not involved getting locked inside the vault and Glen having a gun. "You got a way around the bio scanner and lock panel, be my guest. I'm taking the stairs."

She eased out of the door and into the corridor, searching right and left, before jogging on quiet feet to the stairwell door. It was alarmed, of course. It was for emergency use only. And given all the other alarms she'd set off that night, she really shouldn't worry too much about this one, but this one connected to the full building security, not just the law firm's security, so she was a lot more likely to draw attention if she set this one off.

Last thing she needed, getting humans involved. She was still worried none of the law firm's security were bearing down on her. She'd feel better if she'd had to make a daring escape. This being left to break and enter and escape was making the hairs on her arms rise.

She expected Glen to make a show of heading to the elevator, before following her into the stairwell. He didn't even do that much, just trotted after her.

She made short work of the door alarm—it was standard motion sensor triggered, something she'd dismantled many times before—and slowly pressed the bar to open the door. When no alarm sounded, she smiled and pushed the door open fully.

The stairwell was dark, but lights flickered on when she moved onto the landing, revealing cream walls and black concrete stairs. The stairs circled up two flights to the roof and down the eighteen flights to ground level.

She glanced down the column of space in the center of the stairwell, around which the stairs circled. The lower levels were shroud in darkness. She could barely see the landing below them, and only a little of the landing above them. The roof was as hidden in darkness as the ground.

No one else moving in the stairwell. No other lights triggered.

In an emergency, she assumed all the lights came on. But without triggering the alarm the building probably saved money by keeping the lights on motion detectors only. It was a very handy way for her to know if there were others moving around in the stairwell.

Glen bumped up against her back, looking downward, too. She held on to the rail, and glanced at him. "You looking to jump?" she asked.

He glared at her. "What are you waiting for? Let's get out of here before we run out of luck."

Luck. That's what he wanted her to believe was happening here?

He started toward the stairs heading down. She let him get halfway to the first turn before she went the other way, heading up.

"Hey, where are you going?" he hissed, a sort of shouted whisper that nevertheless echoed in the stairwell.

She didn't bother to answer. She took the steps two at a time, hurrying up to the door that would lead out onto the roof.

Glen's much louder footsteps came after her, a rush of noise that echoed off the concrete walls.

There was another alarm on the roof door. She took the time to disarm it as well, time that gave Glen a chance to catch up. He was puffing and panting as he stumbled up behind her.

"What the hell? How are you planning on getting off the roof?"

"This was always the escape plan. I have an exit. Don't worry."

"I can't fly like your boyfriend," he hissed.

There was a lot of anger in that comment. More than was really called for.

She thought back to the way he'd kept glancing at the king during their meeting. The way he'd gone to the king for help. The way the king had been looking at Glen.

The whole situation stunk, right from the start. Especially the king bringing her in without letting Christopher know about it all.

The locket Glen had retrieved blocked magic. It had to be the reason her magic started working again once they'd retrieved it. Glen's magic should be working now as well.

But he hadn't put the gun away.

"You got a problem with dragon shifters, Glen?" she asked as she pushed open the roof door and studied the flat expanse beyond.

Nothing much up here but extractor fans and a flat, black-tarred surface. The retaining wall around the roof was low, but only two sides were open. The other two butted up directly against the neighboring buildings, both of which were several stories taller than this one.

At the back of the building, there was a gap over an open parking lot with cars in a stacker, six levels high. The front of the building opened up onto the street below. They were half a block over from Lexington, and even at this time of night, the sounds of traffic were clear. The street below, however, was quiet, with crosstown traffic down to a minimum.

Most of the surrounding buildings were dark except for the occasional light in random scattered windows. The building across the street was a sheet of gray-tinted glass with no lights at all showing through.

She made it to the low retaining wall on the side of the building facing the street before she heard the click of Glen's gun.

Myra expected the shot to be fired before she could turn, before he had to look her in the eyes. She'd assumed he'd just shoot her in the back and be done with this.

When he didn't shoot immediately, she turned to face him.

Glen was smiling faintly, his lip lifted in an expression that could more accurately be called a snarling smirk. His tiny, pointless glasses reflected the faint glow of ambient city light.

"So fucking clever," he said. "In and out. If I hadn't triggered that alarm on accident, this would have been done already, wouldn't it?"

"If by *this* you mean the theft, yes. If by *this* you mean shooting me… I can wait longer for that."

He chuckled. "Shame I have to kill you. You really are very good at what you do. But this doesn't work if you survive." He shrugged. "The plan's already screwed up enough as it is. Can't afford to let anything else go wrong."

"Gonna explain the plan or just shoot me?"

He lifted the gun. "Just shoot you."

"I'm going to be dead. Sure you don't want to explain your nefarious plot? I'd like to know why I'm being killed."

"Sorry. Not inclined on discussing it further. Just know, the war will take care of them. You'll be happier dead than watching your boyfriend and his kind die."

Well. None of that sounded good at all. She leaned against the low retaining wall. It came just to the level of her butt, which meant it was really short. Behind her, she could feel the fast breeze of open air, the cold kiss of wide open space, and a long drop.

Glen's eyes narrowed. He lifted the gun so it pointed at her head. "I'm a good shot," he said. "Especially for a wizard. You can't get away."

"Fair enough."

She smiled. Glen frowned. His finger twitched against the trigger.

She leaned back until she felt gravity take her over the edge of the building, was aware of a bullet whizzing past just above her face, heard the sound of the gunshot as she hung for a split second in the open air.

And then she fell.

EIGHT

Now

Air whooshed past Myra as she dropped toward the street. But she didn't freefall for long. Not a high enough building for that.

She heard his wings, the sound of his approach like canvas sails in a breeze, before she felt his arms come up around her, before she could even fire off her grappling hook gun to stop her own fall.

Christopher swooped down to almost road level to catch her, rising up under her. The breathless feeling of his arms snatching her out of the air, the jolt as her drop stopped abruptly. She wrapped her arms around his neck, and the swift beat of his wings pulled them both high up above the rooftops.

She grinned up at the side of his face. "Well hello there. Fancy meeting you here."

He glanced at her, his blue eyes sparking with hints of purple in the night lights. "You okay?"

"Perfect." She held tighter, luxuriating in his warmth. He was shirtless, so his wings could spread out, the partial shift allowing him to keep most of his body in human form as he flew. Before meeting him, she'd had no idea dragon shifters could do this. But it did have its benefits.

The layer of purple and yellow scales over his shoulders and chest were warm and silky. His dark hair was a mess from the flight. If she could see his feet, she knew he'd be barefoot. His jaw was tight, and he looked as angry as she'd ever seen him.

For her part, she'd never been so delighted to see someone in her life. And it wasn't just because he'd swooped her out of the air, stopping her freefall to the hard sidewalk below.

She touched his jaw. "You're okay, too?"

"I've been better. Why didn't you tell me about this job?"

"Honestly? Because your father chose not to tell you. I wanted to see what would happen."

"What happened was you almost got shot."

"Yeah. The gun was a bit of a surprise from a wizard."

He angled high over the building where she and Glen had just robbed the law firm. They both watched as the wizard, looking quite small from this height, hurried back inside. She wondered if he even realized he hadn't killed her. Had he rushed to the edge, to make sure he'd shot her, to make sure she hit the ground? Or did he just shoot and then decide to run?

"Do you know what all this was about?" she asked Christopher as they circled the buildings, waiting for Glen to come out onto the street.

"I found out about the meeting you and my father had with the wizard from a friend in the mansion. It took some digging to find out what the wizard was up to."

"Which was?"

Below them, a few cars moved along the dimly lit cross streets. And if she turned to look over Christopher's shoulder, she'd probably see the louder traffic over on Lexington and Park. But this late, it was remarkably quiet. No horns or loud buses. They were too high up to hear the rumble of the subway, though Christopher might be able to.

The air at this height was cold, sharp. The taste of the city and a chilled breeze off the East

River mingled with Christopher's scent—a mix of dragon musk and a really nice soap tonight. She tightened her arms around his neck, soaking up his warmth. He was really warm tonight. Or maybe she was just cold because she'd nearly been shot and she hated guns.

Or maybe she just really loved Christopher's heat.

"Glen wants to start a war among the shifters. To eliminate them all."

"Ah." She nodded, though she was still a little surprised by the sheer scale of Glen's plan. "One of those wizards." No neutral ground. Either allies or enemies. And Glen was the kind of wizard who was an enemy. "Why the hell did your father arrange for me to help Glen then? Why did Glen go to your father?"

Christopher let out a low, hissing growl that actually made the hairs on her neck tingle. Wow. She wasn't sure that sound boded well for either Glen or the king.

Before he could answer, though, a small shape hurried out of the building onto the street. Glen paused, turned in a circle, ran one direction, looked up at the roof, then searched the street again.

So. He'd thought he'd shot her or at the very least she'd hit the ground and gone splat. He probably should have researched *her* better before getting her involved in all this crap.

Christopher tucked his wings and arrowed toward the street. The feel of the sudden drop, the speed of the air passing as they plunged downward, made Myra gasp. She tightened her grip as her stomach bottomed out and her heart hammered. She had to make an effort not to giggle. The thrill like riding a roller coaster, charging adrenaline and endorphins through her system.

He snapped open his wings and stopped their dive only a few feet above the street. When his feet touched the sidewalk, the landing was gentle and she barely felt the transition between flight and standing. He kept his wings wide behind him, a move that would make him look even larger than he already was.

Glen's back was to them for a split second. Then he turned. Spotted them standing only a few feet away, appearing as if out of nowhere. And stumbled back several steps, nearly landing on his ass in the process. He didn't have the gun in his hand anymore, having tucked it away somewhere. But Myra watched his fingers twitch like he wanted to reach for it.

Given the anger pumping off Christopher in waves of heat, Myra thought it better for Glen's sake that he didn't reach for that gun if he wanted to keep his limbs attached.

Glen looked between Christopher's face and hers, his eyes wide, the panic making his already pale skin sheet white. "How?" he said, though so quietly, she wasn't sure he was actually asking them. Just trying to figure it all out.

"Assuming you could arrange a meeting with my father and endanger the life of someone close to me without me knowing was a mistake," Christopher said.

She resisted the urge to look up at him when he said "someone close to me." He was still holding her in his arms, and she hadn't released his neck so he could put her down. This meant his hands were occupied, which wasn't optimal if Glen decided to pull that gun out. But she also didn't particularly want to let Christopher go now that he was here. And her heart did a funny sort of flutter at the "someone close to me" comment.

The quiet hiss in his voice didn't bode well for Glen, though.

"This won't change anything," Glen said, his eyes wide as he hunted the surroundings for an escape.

"You think my father didn't know what you were trying to do?" Christopher said. "You think he hasn't already started to hunt down your accomplices?"

"He can't stop us. Not all of us."

Myra would sure *love* to know what was going on. But she thought interrupting to ask questions might derail the conversation. If she didn't get answers, soon, though, she was definitely going to grill Christopher about all this later. After kissing him. Maybe after kissing him for a while.

When his hands tightened on her legs and around her lower back, she decided the kissing part would definitely happen before the questions.

"And you can no longer use the locket against us," Glen continued. Which was convenient of him. "It's mine to control now."

"Blocked magic," Myra murmured to Christopher. "At least that's what I think it did. Neither of our magic worked inside the vault until he held it."

"The shifters didn't know what it was," Christopher murmured back. "They knew something in the vault screwed with the illusions they used to disguise their camera, unless they kept the camera at the ceiling. They didn't know which of the things in the vault was responsible for the problem."

"But Glen did." Glen knew which safety deposit box to check, too. That he hadn't told her sooner to open that box so she could use her magic to escape was a question she wasn't sure she'd get an answer to. Maybe he was hoping she wouldn't figure out what the locket did. Not that it would have mattered if he'd always intended on killing her.

"The time of the dragons is done," Glen said with a snarl that he probably thought hid his fear.

"If you come near my people or those I protect again, I'll kill you and hang your body from the top of a Midtown building as a warning to all."

Myra's eyes widened at the threat. She'd never heard Christopher be quite so blunt about killing. She knew he had crisped at least one wizard and some shifters once. The ones who'd kidnapped him and then nearly killed her. She knew killing was within his skill set, so to speak. But the level of violence in his tone made her shiver.

His arms tightened around her, like he was trying to warm her up. Or maybe keep her from running? Not that she'd run from him. She really didn't want to be anywhere else just then but in his arms.

"This isn't over," Glen said. "You can kill me, but more will rise."

"This attempt at starting a war between shifters will not happen. It was a bad plan to begin with. Why do you think there's no shifter security bearing down on you?"

Ah. She'd wondered about that. Obviously, the king had let them know the theft was happening and to let it go. Which meant the shifters were talking, and if the people you were trying to convince to start a war with each other were actually communicating, it was harder to trick them into going to war over a misunderstanding. Bad news for Glen.

Glen hunted the surroundings again, his eyes wide with panic. She didn't have Christopher's sense of smell, but she'd bet he could smell the panic sweat rolling off Glen just then.

"The wizards working with shifters will destroy us all," Glen said. "They need to understand. They need to know."

"Know what?" she asked, curiosity getting the better of her. Again.

"That the shifters will betray us all!" Glen snarled.

And to Myra's utter surprise, he pulled his gun and fired it, so fast, all she could do was blink.

The blink, the hesitation should have cost her. She wasn't usually surprised by people, but Glen had looked so panicked, and he was facing a fucking dragon shifter, that she just assumed he'd run. Especially from Christopher. Especially after attempting to betray the dragon king—even if the king suspected betrayal all along.

She'd made a mistake, assumed Glen would try to get away. And if he attacked, she'd assumed he'd attack with magic. He was a fucking wizard after all.

She had not been expecting the gun. Again.

That mistake, that oversight, should have gotten her shot. Maybe even killed.

Thankfully Christopher didn't suffer from the same oversight.

Or if he did, his hesitation lasted a fraction of the second hers lasted.

He moved so suddenly, and so fast, Myra's stomach bottomed out. A faint nausea gripped her before it was replaced by the thrilling jolt of adrenaline. The same adrenaline she'd gotten freefalling off the side of a building.

Her surroundings blurred. And then they were standing in front of Glen.

Christopher had stepped so close to the wizard, he was inside the man's outstretched arm, the one with the gun. And he didn't give Glen time to adjust to the fact that someone was suddenly standing so close.

Christopher released Myra's legs, and she swung them around to wrap around his waist as he used his now free hand to grip Glen around the neck and lift him off the ground. Christopher's hand was very large compared to Glen's throat. And Christopher was very tall compared to Glen. With his arm stretched straight out in front of him, he held Glen a foot off the ground.

Myra heard the gun clatter to the sidewalk behind them. She patted Christopher's shoulder and dropped her legs. He let her slip down, keeping his arm around her back until she was balanced, then released her.

He never loosened his grip on Glen, who was kicking and wheezing and clawing at Christopher's fingers.

She ducked behind Christopher's wings to retrieve the gun. Once she had the safety on, she stuck it into one of the many pockets in her vest. Then she faced the wizard.

"I'll take that locket now," she said. "I'm not sure what you intended, but you having it is probably bad. And I was paid to steal it, so I think I'll just finish that job."

Glen was too busy trying to breathe to stop her when she took the locket from his pants' pocket. She was a decent pick-pocket, but it wasn't her best skill, so she appreciated that she didn't have to bother.

When she stepped back next to Christopher, pressing her back to his free arm, he finally set

Glen onto his feet, though he didn't take his grip from Glen's throat.

He leaned down and put his face in the wizard's face. "I do not appreciate that you tried to shoot me or my companion. And the only reason you aren't dead is because I do not want to deal with the paperwork tonight. But know this. If you come anywhere near my people, or those I'm close with again, if you attempt to start this nonsensical war, I will find you. I will not be this lenient."

Glen's eyes were starting to roll back into his head. Even on his feet, Christopher's grip left no room for breathing.

"Nod to tell me you understand," Christopher said, very quietly. There was that hiss in his voice again. And the heat pumping off his body was like a furnace at Myra's back.

Glen nodded, proving he wasn't as stupid as Myra thought he might be.

Christopher released him so abruptly he stumbled backward. By the time Glen straightened, she was in Christopher's arms again and they'd leapt into the sky, strong dragon wings beating the air to bring them above the buildings.

She looked down at the shrinking form of the wizard, watched him dropped to his knees on the sidewalk as he presumably sucked in desperately needed oxygen.

"Is he going to…live?" she asked.

"This time," Christopher said, his voice still very deep and that growling hiss quality still lurking beneath the human words. "He tried to shoot you. Twice. I should have killed him."

She patted his cheek. "If he acts up again, you can always kill him then." She considered the side of his face as he banked over the skyscrapers and turned toward the Hudson. "Why didn't you? Out of curiosity."

He flicked her a look, then focused ahead. "I didn't want you to watch me kill someone."

Ah. That was interesting. "You killed before while I was around." But she was unconscious when he had.

"You didn't have to watch."

She nodded, letting this insight into him settle as they flew over the Manhattan skyline.

NINE

Now

Christopher swooped through the tunnel of skyscrapers, moving across the island of Manhattan in the time it would take a bus to move a block in traffic. Faster, really. Myra was only a little surprised that he took her to his apartment—the one she knew about. The one she'd fallen asleep at when they were watching a movie on his patio, snuggled up in comfortable lounge chairs, her belly full of popcorn after a very successful heist.

For some reason, she thought he'd take her to a random rooftop, which is where they'd normally go after a completed heist, or if they needed to talk. But now that she'd been here at his apartment, maybe this was safer.

She didn't mind. She was just happy to see him again.

He set down on the balcony, jogging a little as he came in for a landing, stopping slowly. Greenery filled planters lined the brick wall circling the patio, but most of the space was open. Plenty of room for a partially shifted dragon, maybe even room for his full dragon, though she hadn't seen him in that form yet. There was a light on inside his apartment, so she could just see the marble floored living room beyond the double glass doors leading inside. But the balcony was otherwise dark under the night sky. Giving a sense of seclusion and privacy even though they were surrounded by other buildings.

As the cold night air brushed against her cheeks and neck, she became very aware of Christopher's warmth again. Not just warm. He was hot. Not sweating. His skin was just very… hot. A kind of delicious heat that made her want to groan.

He held her gaze without releasing her and putting her on her feet. She stared back, wondering what he was thinking.

"You're hotter than normal tonight." She touched his shoulders when he raised his eyebrows, a look that made her chuckle. "Your skin, I mean. Is that the anger?"

"Right now? No. That's not why I'm hot."

He released her legs so she slid to her feet, but he held her close, which meant she slid along his body, the glide downward full of friction and intent and possibilities.

"Innuendo?" she asked, feeling a little breathless herself by the time her toes touched the ground. "Or fear."

"Now? Innuendo."

She grinned. "Good." Then she stretched up and met him as he bent his head down to her.

The brush of his lips was gentle at first, gentler than she'd expected, but the minute she sighed, the minute she sank fully against him, tightening her arms around his neck, the kiss went from gentle to hard and urgent. Delicious.

He cupped the back of her head with his big hand, she angled her mouth over his to taste him better. Swiped her tongue against his, tasted that unique flavor she couldn't quite place, but that *tasted* the way Christopher smelled to her. Not just the musk and dragon now either. But that scent of sugar cookies that she sometimes got from him. A rich, vanilla flavor, so delicious she wanted to gobble him up.

Her pulse pounded as her own skin warmed

and heat pooled in her belly and her nerves demanded she rub against him. His groan filled her with a sense of satisfaction, but also left her wanting more.

Yet…

She buried her fingers in his hair, trying desperately to stave off that "yet" and just savor his kiss, his hands on her, his taste, his scent wrapping around her as surely as his heat. She didn't want to think anymore. She'd been thinking about this for weeks now. Ever since meeting him.

And if he was anyone else, she'd throw all caution to the wind and drag him inside to the nearest soft surface where she could strip off the only clothing he currently wore—a pair of dress slacks—and celebrate the fact that she hadn't died tonight with mutual orgasms.

But he wasn't just anyone.

His father had set her up tonight. In a way that could have gotten her killed.

That wasn't something she could ignore. If they kept kissing, if she did take him inside, it took things that one last step toward…something serious. Something his father disapproved of. She couldn't fool herself into thinking sex with Christopher would be a casual fling. Not for her anyway. She was in deep already. Big time crush. Maybe more.

She was already destined to get hurt here. She needed to deal with the fact that his father had set her up to be killed before she let things go any farther.

She still took longer than she should have to ease away from him, to break the kiss, to put some of that cold night air between their very warm bodies.

He held her gaze, looking intent, his jaw tight. He was breathing hard, color highlighted his sharp cheekbones, and his erection had pressed against her belly before she'd stepped back. He still had one hand cradling her head, his fingers tangled in her hair, loosening her bun, but he didn't pull her close again. Just stared down at her, watching her with those sharp blue eyes.

She let him see as much of her, of what she was feeling, as she was able, though years of practice hiding herself from others made that level of vulnerability difficult. Almost impossible.

Finally, he dropped his hold completely and straightened to his full height. Which was significant. She had to crane her neck to look up at him.

"We need to talk," she said.

He nodded. Gestured to the cushion covered lounge chairs. They weren't facing the outer wall of his apartment now, like they'd been for the movie date night, but instead were turned so when they sat, she could see the sky overhead and the building across the street. There weren't many lights, but a few started to pop on as they watched. It must be five in the morning. Getting close to the time people with ordinary jobs that kept ordinary hours would start to wake up.

"Your father tried to get me killed tonight," she said, jumping directly to the big problem.

"I'm not sure he intended for you to die," Christopher said quietly. "More likely this was a test."

"A test?" She scowled at him. "What kind of test?"

"A test to see if you could survive. If you were…worthy."

"Worthing? Of what?"

"His notice." Christopher held her gaze. "Me."

"Isn't that your business? Deciding if I'm worth your time. And my business deciding if *you* are worth *my* time?"

"It is. My father is…bad with boundaries."

She snorted. "He told me, at the meeting when he introduced me to Glen, that he had plans for you and I wasn't part of that. What was he talking about?"

"I have no idea." Christopher's frown and

blank confusion looked sincere enough. "But I'll ask him when I take tonight's situation up with him."

"What will you say? About tonight."

"That if he tries to pull something like this again, with you, I will not let it go passively. Even if he's my father and my king."

"Will that get you killed?"

"No."

He sounded certain. She was…less certain. "You don't have to start a full family war over this. Just let him know I'm not working for him again. Ever. This was the last job. I don't like being made a pawn and he's done that a couple of times now. There's not enough money in his hoard for me to tolerate that."

"I'll tell him."

"Glen wants a war between the various shifters. Why did your father humor him? Why did he even go to your father? Why didn't Glen tell me what the locket did sooner so I could get us out of the vault?"

The way Christopher had talked to Glen, she knew he'd figured out most of the machinations in the background. Now that she was safely away from guns and possibly being arrested for breaking-and-entering, she really did want to know what tonight had been all about. She'd gotten a little of it. But the whys still eluded her.

"Why he didn't tell you what the locket did, I don't know," Christopher said. "Maybe because he didn't understand your skill set and that it would be to his advantage in getting out of the vault."

She smiled a little at that. She didn't mind being underestimated. Gave her the element of surprise.

"As for the war, my sources tell me Glen wants it because he hates shifters, because he thinks wizards are being usurped by them, and because he wants to clear the way for wizards to…rule. To rise to prominence."

"What does a locket that blocks magic have to do with that?"

"He could influence the other wizards, manipulate them if he possessed something that prevented them from using their magic."

"How was all this supposed to start a war between shifters?"

"Your relationship to me, to my father, is… More people know about it now. That you've worked for him a few times. That I'm… That I like you more than a casual acquaintance."

She grinned suddenly. "Really stumbling over how to define this thing between us, aren't you?"

"You able to do any better?"

"Nope." That earned her one of his quick grins, the humor softening some of the hard lines of his angular face. "Keep going." She waved a hand. "Word's getting around that I can be hired by the dragon king. That's probably bad for me. What does that have to do with Glen?"

"Why bad for you?"

"Too many people aware of me. Of who I am. What I do. Hard to be a successful thief when people…see you." He scowled again, but she nudged him. "What does all this have to do with the wizard?"

"From what I could learn, his plan was to have you caught breaking into the vault, trying to escape. The shifters would assume my father arranged the theft—I'm not sure how Glen intended for them to make that assumption—and that would start tension and arguing between the shifters involved. There have been…rumors spreading. Rumors attempting to pit the various shifter groups against each other. The fact that shifters were involved in my kidnapping, and were looking to gain that relic from my father's hoard to turn themselves into monsters only added to those tensions."

He ran a hand through his hair, already messy

and windblown, making the strands stand out in a wild disarray she found extremely sexy.

"I assume Glen is part of those rumors," he continued. "He went to my father because he needed a link between my father and the theft. He wanted the locket. The plan was to kill two birds, so to speak. Get the locket he could use to manipulate his fellow wizards, leave you and the dragon king on the hook for the theft. I'm not sure if Glen intended on killing you from the start."

"He did. He said I needed to die for his plan to work. So, yeah, that was part of it."

Christopher's eyes flared, a dangerous anger tightening his jaw. Almost without thought, she reached out and ran her fingers over his arm, down to his hand, tangling her fingers with his. His expression eased, a little, but a muscle in his cheek still jumped.

"At any rate, he tried to convince my father he wanted the locket because it was dangerous to him in shifter hands. My source in the mansion said Glen was not a great liar, though. He stank of his deceptions. So there was never a chance my father didn't know what was happening."

"For a man who hates shifters and wants to get them fighting, he probably should have done better research on how to keep his nefarious plans secret."

"Probably." Christopher's fingers tightened on hers. "My father went along with it out of perverse curiosity, and to get the locket. But also to see what Glen would do."

"And didn't particularly care if that put me in harms way," she said, nodding. "And he kept it from you because if you knew, you'd have either gone with me or tried to stop the charade before it got started."

"Tried?"

"Well, ultimately, the decisions about which jobs I take or don't take are up to me. Even when I know they're dodgy and the people hiring me are lying to me."

"You knew?"

"I knew the whole thing was a con of some kind. Like your father, I went along with it to find out what was going on."

"You could have been killed." His fingers tightened so hard on hers, she winced. He relaxed his grip instantly, tried to pull his hand from hers.

Her turn to flex her fingers, tightening her hold on him briefly, so he'd know he didn't have to let go if he didn't want to. She waited him out, waited to see if he'd slip his hand from hers or continue to hold her hand.

When he relaxed and left his fingers gently

wrapped around hers, she let out a breath. Her shoulders relaxed.

The rush of uncertainty and fear that brief exchange had caused left her shaken, though. She was really in a lot of trouble with this man. They didn't even have to fuck for her to be fucked here.

She tried to refocus on the other issues, because she wasn't sure how to confront that moment of panic she'd felt waiting to see if he'd let her go.

"I wasn't," she said, clearing her throat because her voice sounded gruff and shaky. "Killed that is. I knew the risks. I knew one or the other of them was trying to play me. I've been doing this for a long time, Christopher."

"You fell off a building. He tried to shoot you. Twice."

"That second time was a bit shocking, I won't lie. I expected him to run. Or try to anyway. But I was ready for the first attempt. I went over the side of that building on purpose."

He let out a low breath. "I saw the grappling hook you tucked away after I caught you."

"It was more fun getting caught."

"You're an adrenaline junkie."

"You're surprised?"

He shook his head.

"Besides." She rolled her lips into her mouth,

studied the building across the street. "I like when you catch me. I like flying with you."

"I like flying with you too."

They sat in silence for a few minutes, both of them staring at the building across the street as the lights came on and the sky overhead turned that deep purple that was almost darker than night before the sun finally peeked over the horizon.

She lifted his hand and brought it to her mouth, giving him a brief kiss without looking at him. Then said, "We have to deal with your father. Before...before this thing between us goes any farther. If it goes any farther. You need to talk to him about...whatever the hell plans these are he has for you. And make sure... Just. Make sure you're free. For this."

"This hard to define thing between us that leaves us both stumbling over our words?"

She laughed and met his gaze. "Exactly." Her smile faded when she said, "I don't want whatever this is to end. But I can't allow it to go on longer if, in the end, it's something you can't...stick with."

She'd almost said commit to, but the whole concept of commitment was foreign to her and she wasn't even sure if that's what she was looking for from him. Especially so soon, so quickly. She just knew she wanted Christopher in her life without worrying that his fate or destiny meant she'd have to give him up whether she liked it or not. Whether they made the decisions to stop seeing each other or not.

"As far as I'm concerned, whatever my father's plans are, they're his idea, not mine. I have no intention of going along with them."

"Okay. That's fair. But you need to make sure he knows that. Because if he doesn't, he might try to set me up to be killed again."

"I won't allow that."

She believed he'd try. He meant what he was saying. But he wasn't omnipotent. If his father really wanted her dead, it was only a matter of time before the king succeeded. Better to just ensure he wasn't trying to kill her.

"I'll talk to him," Christopher said. "I'll make sure the situation is clear."

"As clear as it is to us?" she asked, with a teasing lilt to her voice, trying to take some of the edge off the conversation.

He snorted. His gaze traveled over her face, searching for something in her expression. Then he said, "I'll take you wherever you want to go. But… If you're not too tired, would you like to watch the sunrise with me?"

"Another date?"

"We could call it that."

She nodded and settled back into the lounger, wrapping her arms around his one big arm, cradling it against her because she didn't want to let him go. "A date, it is. I like watching the sunrise."

She especially liked watching the sunrise with him.

THANK YOU

Thank you for reading The Vault Job, Book 4 in the Dragon Thief series! I hope you're enjoying Myra and Christopher's adventures and their slow burn romance. Things really start to heat up in the next two episodes, so I hope you'll keep reading the next story, The Femme Fatale Job. Things are getting interesting.

Once of the fun parts of writing series for me is planting lots of little threads and hints of things that will come back later. It can be a long payoff, but when those things come back around later, it's always so satisfying for me as a writer. This first "season" of the Dragon Thief is that part. I'm planting the seeds, most of which won't grow until later. And I'm looking forward to reaching the point in the overarching story when those seeds start to bloom.

I hope readers will come along for that ride with me.

If you'd like to learn more about my books or try some of my other paranormal romances and urban fantasy romances, you can find more at my website or my bookstore. You can also join my author newsletter for updates on new releases, news, occasional sneak peeks at future stories, free reads, and discounts to my bookstore.

Alternatively, you can follow my author page at BookBub, my author page on Facebook, or my author page at your favorite vendor. Of my various social medias, I'm mostly on Instagram at the moment, where I tend to talk mostly about baking and sporting events, but I will also talk about my books.

Thanks again for reading The Vault Job! I can't wait for you to see what happens next!

~Kat

Don't miss the next story in the
Dragon Thief series!

THE FEMME FATALE JOB

Keep reading for an excerpt!

THE FEMME FATALE JOB
EXCERPT

ONE

yra strolled under the canopy of trees, the bright winter sun filtering down through evergreen branches along the paved path through the middle of Central Park. The Bethesda Fountain was ahead of her, Strawberry Fields behind her, and most of the tourists clumped up in those places so that her stroll was pleasantly people free. The lake to her left peeked out around raised black rocks and greenery, but she didn't take the diverted path to watch the paddle boats. Though it was the middle of winter, the air crisp and frosty at the moment, the lake hadn't frozen, and there were just enough tourists willing to take out a paddle boat even in the cold to keep the service open a little longer.

The Boathouse restaurant wasn't far away, but

she wasn't heading there either. She was ambling. Enjoying the day. No where specific to be.

Waiting for him to find her.

It didn't take him long. He never took very long finding her. In fact, he had an uncanny ability to find her even when she hadn't given him a place to look.

He fell into step beside her, a very tall presence, standing easily a head or more over everyone else around them. He had a good foot and a half on her, which might have been awkward, but she had a real soft spot for tall men.

She had an even softer spot for Christopher.

She glanced at him from the corner of her eye. He was wearing a shirt. A button up business shirt in a soft pink color under a long tan coat. And instead of the dress slacks he normally wore, he was wearing jeans. It was a strange sort of combination, nothing she'd seen him in before. She'd mostly seen him in his flight outfit—pants, no shoes, no shirt so he could shift enough to release his wings. The fact that he was wearing a coat, which she didn't think he needed, and shoes, which he didn't like to wear, made it obvious he was attempting to appear human. Or at the very least, blend in with the humans so he didn't draw too much attention.

Given that he was nearly seven foot tall, it was

impossible for him not to draw attention. But it was always possible the tourists assumed he was a basketball player. This was New York after all. Lots of people could be found walking the paths through the Park.

She bumped his arm with her shoulder, using the excuse of getting that close to him to breathe in his uniquely Christopher scent, that mix of dragon shifter—heat and musk and a very faint hint of brimstone—and some sort of soap that she associated purely with him. No sugar cookie scent at that moment, but she liked when he smelled like this soap of his, too.

"You look good in business casual wear."

"Thank you," he said, his voice deep and rumbling. He tilted his head slightly toward her. "I'm not sure the camouflage is working as well as I'd like."

"It would help if you weren't as tall as some of the trees."

"I can't be sorry for that," he said. "Because you like tall men."

She huffed, tried to swallow her pleased laugh. "I do."

She let her gaze move over the path, skim the scattering of people walking around them. Christopher was drawing stares, but most people looked away quickly. She couldn't tell if they recognized him or not. There weren't any pictures of the royal family allowed in magazines and newspapers. But he did occasionally show up at events with his father, and sometimes in gossip columns. Or at least, he had shown up in the gossip columns at one stage, by name, but he hadn't been in them recently.

Even if people didn't recognize him as the dragon king's son, though, they might still recognize him as a dragon shifter. A lot of the dragon shifters were hard to miss, even in human form.

Not that she'd known that much about them before meeting Christopher. She'd gone out of her way to avoid all things dragon. She mostly stuck to robbing humans, and rich humans at that. Like her soft spot for tall men, she also had a soft spot for stealing from people who already had more than they could keep track of and often didn't even notice when some of their stuff went missing. There was something very satisfying about taking a valuable object from someone like that. And then making herself a small fortune in the process.

Keeping under the radar so she could do her job, though, meant staying under the radar of the movers and shakers in the city. The powerful people.

The dragon king.

She'd blown that up by taking an ill-considered bet and breaking into the king's hoard. A challenge she hadn't been able to resist. The hoard was supposed to be impossible to break into. And if she hadn't been caught standing in the middle of all that wealth, perusing all the fine objects and valuables, looking for something tiny and relatively worthless to take to prove she'd been in the hoard, she wouldn't have ever gotten tangled up with dragon shifters. She would have happily continued to avoid them and everything about them.

But then the king had sent her to rescue his "youngling." That youngling turned out to be a fully grown man. Who was distractingly tall. And strangely attractive in a way that couldn't be described as handsome.

And her life hadn't been the same since.

She regretted getting caught breaking into the king's hoard. She didn't like at all having the dragon king think she worked for him now, or that she was somehow beholden to him. She hated that the dragon king thought of her as one of *his* people.

She did *not* hate that she'd met Christopher.

Unfortunately, his father was a problem. One they needed to deal with before the undefined and very new thing between them went any farther than the few kisses they'd shared and the two technical dates they'd been on. One watching a movie on a screen he'd set up on the balcony of one of his apartments. The second, just a few nights ago, when they'd sat on that same balcony watching the sun rise.

She wrapped her black wool coat around her a little tighter, not because she was cold but because she needed something to do with her hands so she wouldn't automatically reach for his.

"Let's go disappear into the Ramble," she said. "Easier to talk without you drawing all this attention."

He nodded, his own hands stuffed into his pockets as they strolled at a measured pace to a section of forest that spread across the middle the Park. Winding dirt paths twisted through thick, dense woodlands, though the oak and maple limbs were bare now, giving the area a lovely stark effect. Dark rocky outcroppings rose up around corners in the bending paths, and sun flittered down to the fern and vine underbrush.

They followed the paths, encountering a handful of birders as they moved deeper into the woods. The feeling of being in a city disappeared. Even the smell was all nature, dirt and trees, dried leaves and pine. Myra could almost believe they were walking through the woods in Upstate New York, far away from everything they had to deal with.

When she was certain they were alone, with no random people around the next bend, she broached the reason for this meeting. "What did your father say?"

Christopher's mouth tightened. "Not as much as I wanted. He refused to acknowledge what he told you about having plans for me. He won't admit to any such thing. He's a stubborn old bastard." This last said under his breath, with a twist of annoyance to his mouth.

"Did he tell you I lied about what he'd said?" She was more curious than offended. The king was used to manipulations and lies. She wouldn't put it past him. Especially since he'd made it clear he disapproved of her relationship with Christopher, even as he kept attempting to make her one of his "humans," one of the humans known to work for him.

"He didn't, actually. He claimed you misremembered."

"Huh. I would have expected him to just say I lied."

"I found the hedge interesting, too. He likes you."

"No, he doesn't. He set me up to be killed."

The last job the king had hired her for had put her in the way of a wizard who'd tried to shoot her. Twice. That wasn't usually something a person who liked you did.

"*Like* is maybe a strong word. Admire. He admires you. And I was right. That job was a test. A test he claims he thought you'd pass."

"If I survived, I'm worthy, right?" She snorted, a sardonic sound of her own.

She didn't want the king's admiration or to be worthy in his attention. She didn't give two fucks about whether he found her worthy or not. She just wanted him to leave her alone now.

"That fits with his way of thinking," Christopher said on a sigh.

"And when you told him I'm not working for him again?"

Christopher let out a hissing sort of growl. A sound she associated with dragon shifters. A sound no human made. "He smiled," Christopher said. "He claimed you'd change your mind."

"Wow. He's never been so wrong about anything before. I do not intend on changing my mind."

"I know." Christopher's shoulders hunched as he scowled down at the dirt path, his hands still firmly in his coat pockets. "He mentioned something…"

"Another job?" She narrowed her eyes at him.

"Not…technically. But, it's a situation that…" He trailed off and looked out at the trees, turning his face away from her.

But not before she saw the color rise in his cheeks, the red blush coloring his high, sharp cheekbones.

He was blushing. That could only mean one thing.

"There's a damsel in distress, isn't there?"

She pressed her lips together so she wouldn't grin. He was sensitive about this particular soft spot of his. Her attempt not to smile failed miserably, though, so she just gave in. She loved that he was a dragon with a soft spot for damsels in distress. In fact, it was one of the things about him she liked the most.

But the character trait got him razzed by the other dragons. The trait had also been exploited by the people who'd kidnapped him.

"There might be," he mumbled.

"You know he's manipulating you, right? To get you to do what he wants you to."

"Yes." Still a mumble.

"But you'd like my help saving this damsel anyway because this is a damsel in distress situation?"

"Yes." He admitted with a sigh.

She bumped his arm again. "For you, I'll help. But not for the king. For you."

Without looking at her, he took one hand out of his pocket and stretched it out to her. She only hesitated a beat before taking hold of his hand and twinning her fingers with his. His hand was so much bigger than hers, he completely engulfed her. But he was also exceptionally gentle with that size and strength. She never worried about him hurting her.

He squeezed gently and she felt his muscles relaxing as they walked.

"My father *claims* he will no longer attempt to hire you," Christopher said. "He *says* he understands you prefer your independence and do not want to accept the protection of the dragons."

"Protection?" She snorted. The king had a funny idea of the word "protection" if he thought sending her on a job to get killed qualified.

"He hasn't given up on trying to pull you into his permanent employ," Christopher said. "He'll likely keep trying. But for now, he's pretending to let you go your own way."

"I see." She did. It was a game for the king. But...

Where did that leave her and Christopher?

Don't miss Myra and Christopher's
most dangerous adventure to date!

THE FEMME FATALE JOB

Out now!

Join Kat's Newsletter

Stay Up-to-Date

On all Kat's News, Updates, and fun extras

New Subscriber Get Two Exclusive Stories Just for Signing up!

bit.ly/KatSimonsNewsletter

KatSimonsBooks

Mystery

Urban Fantasy

Romance

And More!

THE DRAGON THIEF
The Dragon Thief Series
Kat Simons
SEASON ONE

Books By Kat Simons

Dragon Thief Series

<u>Season One</u>

Dragon Thief

The Chicago Job

The Poisons Book Job

The Vault Job

The Femme Fatale Job

The Scavenger Job

<u>Season Two</u>

The Crown of Kingship Job

The Green Scroll Job

The Payback Job

Pick Your Genre Collections

Who Steals a Dragon

The Cary Redmond Series

* The Trouble Black Cats and Demons * The Trouble with Ghouls and Serial Killers * The Trouble with

Leopard Queens and Shifter Wars * The Trouble with Baby Gods and Vampires * The Trouble with Magic and Faery Curses * The Trouble with Wizards and Old Enemies * The Trouble with Death and Demon Gods

The Cary Redmond Series Box Set Books 1-3

Cary Redmond Short Stories

* When Cary Met Jaxer * When Cary Met Pickles * When Cary Met Marianne * When Cary Met Lucy * When Cary Met Angie * Cary and Deacon (Try to) Go on a Date * Date Night Take Two * Third Date's the Charm * Cary vs the Goblin King * Dinner with the Joneses * Cary and the Cursed Jack-O'-Lantern * Cary and the Demon Witch * Cary Goes to Hawaii * Cary Holidays * Cary and Dragons and Goblins * Cary's Galentine's Day * Cary at the Haunt and Howl * Cary's Leprechaun Troubles * Cary's Beltane Night Out *

When Cary Met the Good Guys (Collection 1)

Dates, Dinners, and Other Disasters (Collection 2)

Witches and Weavers and Ghosts, Oh Boy (Collection 3)

A Very Cary Holiday (Collection 4)

Romancing the Leopard: A Tiger Shifters-Cary Redmond Crossover Novel

Tiger Shifters Series

* Once Upon a Tiger * Along Came a Tiger * Here There Be Tigers * Her Tiger To Take * To Tempt a Tiger * Down Will Come Tiger * To Catch a Tiger * What a Tiger Wants * Taming Her Tiger

Tiger Shifters Series Vol 1 (Books 1 - 3)

Tiger Shifters Series Vol 2 (Books 4 - 6)

Seven Families Series

Wolf Family

Darkness in Stone

Redemption in Stone

Fated in Stone

Wolf in Stone: A Seven Families Box Set, Books 1-3

Demon Witch Series

Howling Dreadful

Moonlit Strange

Bone Lantern Witch

Spiderweb Witch

Storm Shadow Witch

Darkling Mist Witch

Joan of Kerry Series

Joan of Kerry: Joan and the Abhartach

Joan and the Leprechaun

Joan and the Kraken

Joan and the Selkie

Joan and the Goblins

Haunts and Howls Collections

Haunts and Howls and Guardian Spells

Haunts and Howls Where Demons Dwell

Haunts and Howls and Jesters Bells

Haunts and Howls and Fairy Dales

*Tombstone Wizard * The Unshattered Sword *
Destiny Through the Cats Eyes * Going Out of
Business: Everything's for Sale * Anger Management *
Demonic Dates * Friday's Curious Shop * The Museum
of Small Art's Everyman * Burning Inside a Stone
Circle * Bored Questless * I Just Ate a Bug * Ting Ling
* Sophie Saves the World * Black Water Hawthorns
*To Dance in Fallow Fields at Midnight *

MORE BOOKS BY KAT SIMONS

Contemporary Romances

Designed for You

Poinsettias and Possibilities

Mystery and Thrillers

Ross and O'Neill Adventures

Galileo's Pendulum

Percy James Mysteries

Movies May Murder

Cookies Can't Crime

Diamonds Do Damage

Replicas Risk Ruin

Vacation Deadly: An Action Adventure Thriller
Collection

About the Author

Kat Simons earned her Ph.D. in animal behavior, working with animals as diverse as dolphins and deer. She brought her experience and knowledge of biology to her paranormal romance and urban fantasy fiction, where she delights in taking nature and turning it on its ear. She writes urban fantasy, contemporary fantasy, and paranormal romance in series which combine action adventure, the otherworldly, and a frequent dose of sexy romance.

The newest book in her bestselling romantic urban fantasy series about Protector Cary Redmond, The Trouble with Shifters and Fae Courts, sees a new direction for the intrepid Protector, her sexy leopard shifter mate, and the entire crew. Kat also launched a new novella length Paranormal Romance series that follows the adventures of a magical thief and the dragon shifter prince she just can't seem to shake—and really doesn't want to. The first season of the Dragon Thief series released throughout 2024.

Season Two begins in 2025 with The Crown of Kingship Job.

For something a little different, Kat also publishes fantasy, science fiction, and the occasional hockey romance under the name Isabo Kelly (https://www.isabokelly.com).

After traveling the world, living in places like Hawaii, Germany, and Ireland, Kat now lives in New York City with her family and a library's worth of books.

For more on Kat and her future books

Website: https://www.katsimons.com/
Newsletter: https://bit.ly/KatSimonsNewsletter

KatSimonsBooks

https://www.katsimonsbooks.com
https://www.TheCafeatKatSimonsBooks.com

Social Media

Facebook Page: https://www.facebook.com/
KatSimonsAuthor
BookBub: https://www.bookbub.com/authors/kat-
simons
Bluesky: https://bsky.app/profile/katsimons.bsky.
social
Instagram: https://www.instagram.com/isabokelly/
Threads: https://www.threads.net/@isabokelly